---- ★ ----

As she rounded the French doors that opened into the sunroom, she saw the foot. She stopped. Her stomach tightened. She listened. Not a sound. The foot was bare, attached to a hairless leg and it wasn't moving. She wanted to run but she couldn't move. After a ten-second eternity, she forced herself to edge forward.

She turned the corner. Only her years as a daughter who had butchered her father's deer kept her from passing out. And it wasn't the red of berries dappling the sofa. And if the porcelain lamp that was as smashed as the widow's skull was the one Nora had intended to put up for auction—that could never happen.

EBay does not list weapons.

---- ----

DEAD MADONNA

VICTORIA HOUSTON

W🌐RLDWIDE®

TORONTO • NEW YORK • LONDON
AMSTERDAM • PARIS • SYDNEY • HAMBURG
STOCKHOLM • ATHENS • TOKYO • MILAN
MADRID • WARSAW • BUDAPEST • AUCKLAND

For Ron and Linda—
Thanks for remarkable insight into the criminal mind
and a welcoming home away from home.

DEAD MADONNA

A Worldwide Mystery/October 2008

First published by Bleak House Books.

ISBN-13: 978-0-373-26651-7
ISBN-10:   0-373-26651-0

Printed in U.S.A.

One never knows, do one?
—Thomas "Fats" Waller

Water is the one substance from which the earth can
conceal nothing; it sucks out its innermost secrets
and brings them to our very lips.
—Jean Giraudoux (1882–1944),
The Madwoman of Chaillot

A true Conehead Madonna trout fly is a challenge to tie:
The thread must be stolen from a spider,
The feathers from the wings of an angel.

ONE

ROBBIE MORIARTY HUNCHED over to squeeze through the doorway of the houseboat. The morning sun hit his eyes. He winced. The vertigo worsened. Making sure to lean far over the railing, he heaved his guts out. Even in misery, he was careful not to splatter the pontoons gleaming beneath him.

The boat lurched forward, then lurched again. Though he could hear the soft whirr of the trolling motor, the boat went nowhere. And the jerking motion didn't help his nausea.

Robbie pressed his head into his hands, fingers hard against his eyeballs—anything to wipe away the brutal headache. He took a swig from a can of Mountain Dew MDX, tipped his head back and gargled. Without opening his eyes, he turned his head to the left and spit, then waited, eyes still closed, to hear the soft plop on the water. The boat lurched as he took another swig, gargled, tipped his head to the right this time, and spit. Another soft splatter. He forced his eyes open. Ouch. The day looked too good for how he felt.

Beneath the boat, the lake was so clear he could see every ridge and hollow in the boulders and sunken logs that appeared to be no more than three to four feet beneath the surface. Aware that water was a magnifier, he found it hard to tell how deep the channel was here. Another lurch convinced him the boat had run aground. Were they too far to the right? Had they hit a sandbar?

Whatever you do, don't turn on the inboard, he cautioned himself. Last thing he needed was to wreck yet another propeller. That would make three this summer. The old man angry was no fun.

He inhaled through his nose and exhaled slowly, steadying himself against the rail. Vomiting had definitely helped—he could tolerate fresh air without the urge to heave. Robbie shifted his feet to see if the deck of the boat would stay where it belonged.

Taking one last swig from the can, he tossed the empty container into the lake and swished the Mountain Dew through his teeth. He was just about to spit when, in his peripheral vision, he caught a streak of white in the water off to his right. He leaned out and over the railing, the better to see. The boat lurched and he grabbed the rail to keep from going over.

What on earth was stuck under the boat? Again he leaned forward, forward… There! He saw it again. A scarf?

Maybe one of the girls from the party lost it? Or could it be Troy's jockey shorts? The white ones with "home of the whopper" emblazoned in red across the butt. No matter how often you tell that guy to keep his pants on…

The white thing wafted forward again and this time he saw a trace of red. He did his best to focus despite the stale booze flooding his brain. Still, it took a few seconds to register that the red spots he saw had nothing to do with

Troy's whopper. They tipped the fingers of the slender arm that belonged to someone hidden under the boat.

Robbie screamed.

THREE MILES UP THE LAKE, Audrey Moriarty's cell phone shattered the silence of the sunny, windless morning with a crescendo of "Rhapsody in Blue." Reaching over her breakfast plate for the phone, she picked it up and leaned back in her chair—only to flinch and hold the phone away at the unexpected blast of her stepson's hoarse voice. "Where's Dad? Goddammit, Audrey, put Dad on. We got a girl stuck under the boat. I think…" His voice cracked, he gagged and she could hear him vomiting.

"Hold on, Robbie," Audrey said, pausing, her eyelids drooping low in thought before she handed the phone across the table to the man sitting there, his Sunday *New York Times* a shield between them. "It's for you, dear."

Then she stood, picked up her plate and let herself through the sliding glass door. She caught her reflection in the window. She was a stylish, slim-hipped woman well aware that many of Bert's friends were convinced he had made a mistake when he married for the third time. She wasn't his type: too thin, too cool and not the whiskey-voiced good-time girl he deserved.

Audrey stepped into the kitchen of the overbuilt full-log house that she was preparing to leave for good. She set her plate in the sink, which faced the deck, and watched as the blood rose in her husband's face.

Yes, she was just in time. The papers would be served when Bert returned to the office. Her lawyer had completed the paperwork earlier that week. So whatever was going on with that stupid boy, the stupid houseboat and whoever the stupid girl was that got herself in trouble—it would all be Bert's problem. The fool. He deserved it.

She couldn't help smiling.

TWO

WITH A YANK ON THE emergency brake, Sharon Donovan parked her van in front of the storage barn that had been built to match the sprawling white clapboard lake house. Jumping down from the driver's seat, she hurried around to the back of the van. She threw open the doors and checked to be sure she hadn't forgotten the stack of old quilts she would need to protect the furniture.

Stepping back, hands on her hips, she ran down a mental list of anything else she might need. Nothing. The sunny day took care of any worry about rain. Sharon checked her watch. Right on time.

Bouncing down the flagstone walk that led to the main house, she resisted the urge to skip. Instead, she let a swell of gratitude rush her through a Hail Mary—something she had taken to doing twenty times a day since eBay had changed her life.

Not only was her income triple what she had been making as a high school English teacher, but she was working with the love of her life: antiques. She still found it hard to believe she could set her own hours—plus the running around was great for weight loss. Already she weighed less than she had in years: two hundred and fifty pounds!

The back door to Nora Loomis's house was ajar. Sharon poked her head in and said, "Hey! Nora? It's Sharon. I'm here." No answer.

Pushing the door open, she walked onto the airy, plant-filled porch that had just been totally renovated to allow for year-round use—part of what Nora referred to as the "extreme makeover" of her entire home. "Better than therapy," the newly widowed woman had said when they first talked.

"I have so much of Jerry's parents' old stuff that I can't wait to get rid of," Nora had said during their phone conversation a week earlier. "But I just took a job in the call center at that new medical supply company and I don't have the time to deal with all this."

And so they had arranged for Sharon to stop by the house, assess the value of the antique Fiesta dinnerware, two Victorian sofas, an assortment of mahogany end tables, three porcelain table lamps that Nora was pretty sure dated back to the 1920s if not earlier, and her late husband's muskie rods and tackle.

Assuming Nora would be comfortable with her estimates, Sharon would take photos, write descriptions and put everything up for auction on eBay. As the items sold, Sharon would handle the shipping. For her efforts, she could keep thirty percent, which was more than fine with her.

The lamps sounded so intriguing, she was considering buying those herself and putting them up for auction with a reserve. She wanted to run that by Nora but she was pretty sure it would work; Nora had said she wanted her money as soon as possible. Sharon was open to the risk. She had learned that if you're willing to take your time, antique lamps can sell for a lot more than most people expect.

"Nora! I'm here," Sharon said, raising her voice as she crossed the porch to the door leading into the kitchen. Nora's car was parked in the circular drive so she had to be somewhere. I'll bet she's down in the basement, Sharon thought, moving toward a door that looked like it might lead there. Nope. It opened to a pantry. She turned around. Looking down the hall to her right, she caught a glimpse of the living room.

"Nora? It's Sharon—I'm h-e-r-e…" The last thing she wanted to do was surprise the woman and scare her to death. Twice she called out as she walked toward the living room. The hall opened into the west end of a long, formal living room, which ran parallel to the shoreline of the Wisconsin River, visible through tall, leaded windows.

Sharon's first thought was how lucky Nora was to be able to keep this place. Her second thought was what a mess!

Hands on her hips, she looked around. If she didn't know better, she'd have thought a family of squirrels had moved in. The seat cushion from one of the two Windsor chairs in front of the fireplace was on the floor. The magazine table next to the chair was at a cockeyed angle. Fireplace tools lay across the beige carpet— certain to leave black streaks.

Farther down the room, a lovely Oriental jar lay on its side on a small love seat. Good thing *that* hadn't hit the floor. On the floor beside the love seat, a full waste-basket was tipped over, scattering dirty Kleenex, crumpled newspapers and cracker crumbs across the rug.

Honest to Pete! What is it with these women who depend on cleaning ladies and decorators to keep their rooms straight? Have they forgotten how to run a vacuum cleaner?

Sharon shook her head. If this was how she kept house, Nora might not be such a good client after all. Any furniture to be sold needed to be in pristine condition. Pristine.

Sharon grimaced. If this was how the upstairs furnishings were treated, what would the condition of the antiques stored in the basement be? Moldy?

"Nora," she called out, her tone sharper this time. Another hall led toward the bedroom wing. But as she started in that direction, Sharon caught sight of a sofa in the sunroom located at the far end of the living room. Oh, it took her breath away.

Even from a distance she could tell the British influence: an elegant curve to the wooden legs—and the fabric! Mint-green leaves against a rich cream background dappled with sprigs of something red. Holly berries, perhaps? The morning sun highlighted the sheen in the fabric and Sharon bet anything it was damask. Silk damask. Brother, what a sofa like that would bring on eBay… Actually, it would look great in her home.

Tiptoeing across the room, she decided to try it out before Nora showed up and caught her sitting down. As she rounded the French doors that opened into the sunroom, she saw the foot. She stopped. Her stomach tightened. She listened: not a sound. The foot was bare, attached to a hairless leg and it wasn't moving. She wanted to run but she couldn't move. After a ten-second eternity, she forced herself to edge forward.

She turned the corner. Only her years as a daughter who had butchered her father's deer kept her from passing out. Nora was not going to be selling on eBay. And it wasn't the red of berries dappling the sofa. And if the porcelain lamp that was as smashed as the widow's skull was the one she had intended to put up for auction—that could never happen.

Ebay does not list weapons.

THREE

SHARON FORCED HERSELF to stay near Nora until the Loon Lake police arrived. Partly because she knew it was the right thing to do, partly because she was terrified. What if the person who did this was still in the house? Or watching from outside? Someone who might follow her next?

"I am so afraid," she sobbed to the police dispatcher whom she had reached on her cell phone.

"Of course you are," said the woman on the switchboard. "That's why I'll keep this line open and you tell me if you see or hear anything. Okay? I want you to calm down if you can. Chief Ferris knows where you are—she is on her way as we speak.

"My name is Marlene," she continued, her tone matter-of-fact, "and I need your name and address." The practical request forced Sharon to get a grip. With the phone clutched to her ear, she tiptoed across the sunroom to an antique wooden rocker, the only piece of furniture not splattered with blood. Every few seconds she checked the figure on the floor, hoping. But the foot did not move. She refused to look higher.

"Good news," said the dispatcher. "Chief Ferris just turned onto Loomis Road…"

"Great…" said Sharon in a low whisper, trying her

best to sit still in the rocker though her body insisted on shaking.

"Yeah," said Marlene. "It'll be just a moment now— Say, don't you wonder how you get a road named after you?"

"I imagine your family owned the property when the road was put in," said Sharon, grateful for the diversion.

"Yep," said Marlene, "or your old man was on the county board, doncha know."

As she spoke, Sharon heard the swish of a car followed by footsteps running up to the back door. But it wasn't until she saw the woman in the khaki police uniform running through the living room toward her, right hand on the gun holstered at her hip, that she dared to say, "She's here, Marlene—thank you so much!" and clicked off her phone.

"Any sign of other parties?" said Chief Ferris, looking first at Sharon, then down the hall leading to the bedroom.

"No. Just me and…" Sharon choked, unable to say Nora's name. "Huh, huh, huh," she heaved. "I'm…I'm… I'm so sorry…don't mean to break down…"

"Take a deep breath," said the woman, whose daughter had been one of Sharon's best students years earlier. She laid a sympathetic hand on Sharon's shoulder. "Are you okay?" As she spoke, a tall young man in a police uniform crossed the living room toward them. "This is my deputy, Todd Martin."

"I'm—ah, well, one thing I'm not is 'okay,'" said Sharon with a weak laugh, as she pushed herself up from the rocker. "Not okay at all." She wiped at her eyes, determined to settle down. "Yes, I know Todd. I used to teach with his mother. Sharon Donovan, Todd." She thrust a hand toward each of the officers then stepped backward into the living room, her body still trembling.

"I'll need you here for a while, Mrs. Donovan," said Chief Ferris. "And, please, don't move around. We don't want to disturb anything we don't have to. So I need you to stay right where you are for the next few minutes."

"It's 'Miss,'" said Sharon, "or Ms.—whatever. I'm no longer married."

Chief Ferris nodded. She turned away from Sharon to study the body and the conditions in the sunroom. She looked back at Sharon. "I have to ask you a few questions but we need to secure the house and the crime scene first."

She gave her deputy a quick glance. "I don't need Pecore to tell me this is a homicide. You know the drill, Todd." Her tone was so crisp and authoritative that Sharon momentarily allowed herself the feeling that life was back under control.

The young officer waved the roll of yellow tape in his right hand. "Yep, I'll do a walk-through of the house first, Chief, just to be sure we have no one else on the premises. Then I'll head up to the driveway," he said.

"Does that mean you have to impound my van?" said Sharon, worry in her voice.

"I don't think so," said Chief Ferris. "If that's you on the blacktop by the barn, you may be parked far enough away from the house. How many times have you gone back and forth?"

"I only just walked in. Right away I saw…"

"Then I doubt we'll need your vehicle, but Todd will check. Now why don't we step outside to talk," she said, opening the door to the garden off the sunroom. "The less we disturb in here, the better."

"Do you mind if I call my next appointment and let them know I'll be late?" said Sharon, gesturing with her cell phone.

"Go right ahead," said Chief Ferris with a wave of her hand as she started down flagstone stairs leading toward the river. Pausing halfway, her back to Sharon, she pulled a long, narrow notebook from the back pocket of her khakis and stood jotting notes.

Three times Sharon tried punching in the number for the client she was scheduled to meet at noon. Not only were her hands still shaking but as she started to speak, her throat closed and the only noise she could make was a hoarse sob. Chief Ferris turned at the sound and skipped back up a couple steps. "Sharon," she whispered, "a deep breath." Sharon did as she was told. She found her voice.

"Mallory?" she said. "I'm, ah, I'm running late, maybe another hour or so. Is that a problem for you?"

"Not at all—but is something wrong?" said Dr. Paul Osborne's oldest daughter, who had taken the call on her own cell phone from where she was standing in her father's basement.

"Just a bad start to the day," said Sharon, with a weak smile at Chief Ferris. "Tell you about it when I see you."

"Please take your time, Sharon. Erin and I have our hands full sorting through all Mom's stuff—we had no idea how much junk was down here. You come when you can or call back if we need to do it later, okay? I'm at Dad's through the weekend."

"THAT WASN'T PAUL OSBORNE'S DAUGHTER you just spoke to, was it?" said Chief Ferris, concern in her voice as Sharon slipped her cell phone back into her pocket. "I don't mean to be nosy but there aren't many people named Mallory around here."

"Yes…I'm meeting her and her sister, Erin," said Sharon, wondering what could possibly be wrong with that. "They want me to sell their mother's china on eBay."

"In that case, I would appreciate it if you would do me a favor when you get there—give Doc a message for me?"

"I don't know if he'll be there or not," said Sharon. "Mallory is the one who has made all the arrangements. But I'll be happy to if he—"

"Tell him I have to cancel our plans for tonight."

Before Sharon could answer, the cell phone on Chief Ferris's belt rang. "Yes, Marlene?" Again the no-nonsense tone that Sharon found reassuring.

"Are you serious?" said the police chief, her voice terse. "Wait—let me get this straight. You're telling me our overpaid coroner took the week off to play his accordion at a polka convention? When the hell did he decide to do this? Why didn't he tell *me* he was leaving town?"

Sharon couldn't make out what was said next, but the mollified look on Chief Ferris's face answered the question. "Oh…well, my fault. The memo's in my box, huh? That's what I get for relying on e-mail. All right, Marlene, hold tight while I rethink what's happening here because I've got two fatalities under questionable circumstances… What's that?"

She paused to listen. From where she stood, Sharon could hear a high-pitched chatter. Irritation flashed across Chief Ferris's face. "Oh, he has, has he? Well, you tell Mr. Bertram Moriarty I don't care *how* much he pays in property taxes or *when* his plane leaves for

Chicago—he does not budge from that boat until I get there. No…one…leaves.

"And, given what I see here, I'd say it will be a good hour or more until I can get there. I can't send Roger because he's got his hands full with that three-car accident in the Loon Lake Market parking lot. Plus I don't want him there. So tell those people to hold their horses.

"Now, Marlene, I need a coroner and the Wausau boys ASAP. I'll give a call to Chuck Meyer at the Wausau Crime Lab—but will you please reach Doc Osborne and brief him on the situation? Thank you. Give him this address and ask him to meet me here as soon as possible. I'll need him here and at Moccasin Lake."

Chief Ferris hadn't even clipped her phone back onto her belt before it rang again. "He's not answering? Damn. Okay, call Ray and ask him to walk over and see if he can find him. I know Doc was planning to fish with his grandson this morning."

Again her phone rang within thirty seconds. "No answer from Ray, either? Jeez, Louise—what else can go wrong! Try Ray at the cemetery—if we're lucky he's running the backhoe."

IT WASN'T UNTIL forty-five minutes later, when Sharon was safe in her van and markedly more calm, that it dawned on her: Chief Ferris and Doc Osborne dating? Really.

Her right eyebrow arched. She liked that thought. Sharon wasn't single by choice and she had every intention of dropping another fifty or sixty pounds. If a woman like Lewellyn Ferris—strong, sturdy and so forthright (to put it mildly)—could attract a man as good-looking, as distinguished as Dr. Paul Osborne… Hmmm, maybe there was hope for Sharon Donovan. With that happy thought, she reached for her cell phone—time to let the Osborne sisters know she was on her way.

FOUR

THE ROWBOAT ROCKED LIGHTLY on the wake generated by a passing Jet Ski. Seated with his legs akimbo, Paul Osborne speared the angleworm with an authority gained from thirty years of practicing dentistry—a profession geared to small spaces and sharp instruments.

He did not work in solitude: two sets of eyes were riveted on his fingers as he manipulated the angleworm—a premium specimen one-eighth of an inch thick and fired with the energy of a chipmunk. Mission accomplished, Osborne held up the worm, looped twice on a hook sized for bluegills, for his companions to examine.

"The trick is to hide the hook but leave plenty of worm to wriggle and draw the fish in," he said, twisting the hook so they could see both sides. Seated opposite Osborne in the boat was his youngest grandchild, Cody, who brushed a shock of straight, white-blond hair out of his eyes to study the doomed worm with the concentration of a research scientist. Cody's older sister, Mason, her kayak bumping up against the boat, leaned so far forward to get a good look that she nearly tipped over.

Steadying the kayak, she said with a pout, "Grandpa, I get to go fishing next, right? Not fair Cody gets to go and I can't."

"Part of his birthday present," said Osborne, his tone

matter-of-fact. He refused to be bullied by a nine-year-old. Cody beamed and reached for the rest of his gift, which was connected by fishing line to the worm: a graphite fast-action St. Croix spinning rod outfitted with an Omega Reel that needed only the pressure of a small thumb on its rubber button to shoot line without a hitch. Osborne might be out a hundred and twenty-five bucks for the rig, but he was determined to see Cody spend his sixth birthday fishing with the ease of an expert.

Two days earlier, frustrated to the point of cursing, Osborne had trashed the cheap rod the boy had inherited from his non-fishing father. Together, grandfather and grandson visited Ralph's Sporting Goods, where they tested rods for a good half hour.

"Cody," Osborne had counseled, "if there's one lesson in life you need to remember, it's this. Never hesitate to put your money into good tools. You will never regret it."

OSBORNE CERTAINLY DIDN'T regret it. Money spent on good tools had changed his life. First, there was the reputation he earned over the thirty years of his dental practice, thanks to an excellent education, a love for his profession—and the finest instruments he could afford. Even as he retired, he held on to those instruments, refusing to bend to the demands of his late wife that they be sold with the practice. It was a decision that, four years later, would indeed change his life.

Then, there was the money spent on fishing tackle: spinning rods and lures that were more than just tackle—they were a means of escape. Escape from his marriage to a woman who spent twenty-five years responding with the same three words on hearing his voice on the telephone: "Oh…it's you." No hiding *her* disappointment.

EVEN THE EXPENSIVE fly rod that he purchased not knowing if he would enjoy fishing *in* water rather than *on* water had been a serendipitous investment. Though he didn't have an opportunity to use it until after Mary Lee's death, it *really* changed his life.

Thanks to that fly rod, he would enjoy extraordinary evenings in breathtaking streams, followed by enchanting nights in the arms of a woman he had never expected to meet: *a woman who fished.* And one who was so impressed with his willingness to spend money on a good rod—not to mention take instruction from a female—that she agreed to teach him the basics of fly-fishing. To their mutual surprise, they caught more than trout: each hooked the other by the heart.

THE LATE-MORNING SUN fell warm across Osborne's shoulders. Overhead the air was still. Wisps of white cotton clouds brushed a Dresden blue sky. A perfect July day. Resting his hands on the oar handles, he let the boat drift, pulling Cody's bobber along.

He couldn't help but congratulate himself for spending time and money to restore the old Rhinelander rowboat, a sturdy antique that he had inherited from his father. The money spent on the boat, the new spinning rod—even the buck fifty on angleworms—all added up to a look on his grandson's face that he couldn't buy.

Having cast a respectable twenty feet out from the boat, the youngster sat perfectly still, breath held and eyes fixed on the gentle rocking of the red-and-white bobber. Across from him, Osborne sat just as still but with peace and gratitude brimming in his heart.

"Grandpa?" Mason broke the silence from where she had let her kayak drift down the shoreline. Osborne glanced her way. In her white, one-piece swimsuit, orange life vest and blue-green kayak, she was as colorful as a water lily in full bloom. Waving her paddle, she said, "Did Mom tell you we found the secret passage yesterday? We went all the way up to Hidden Lake. Found secret treasure, too, Grandpa.

"I wanted to bring you a present 'cause all the secret stuff is so cool, but Mom said no. She thinks it has to belong to somebody but I know she's wrong. Why would you put stuff way out in the woods? So Mom and I made a deal—if it's still there next summer, I get to keep it. And I know right where to find it, too, but you have to be in a kayak or a canoe 'cause it's pretty shallow. Too shallow for your fishing boat, you know." She spoke with an authority that made her grandfather grin.

Keeping an eye on Cody's bobber, Osborne said, "Good for you, Mason. You're wise to listen to your mother and I'm impressed with your kayaking. You're becoming quite the expert, young lady."

"Yep," said Mason, tilting her head as she grinned with pride, "that's what Mom said." She dipped her paddle, pointing the kayak toward the rowboat. Osborne was about to warn her not to crowd Cody's bobber but decided to keep his mouth shut, trusting she would use her head and not need a scolding.

MASON WAS HIS DAUGHTER Erin's middle child. Overshadowed by twelve-year-old Beth, an excellent athlete and student, and by her little brother, Cody, the first boy and an exuberant easy-to-love child, Mason had a habit of going to extremes to get attention. Osborne cut her more slack than her parents did; he knew just how she felt.

He, too, had been overshadowed. Mary Lee's attitude toward him had changed after Erin's birth. The intimacies of their early years together seemed to vanish overnight. Instead, Osborne found himself treated as an irritating but necessary appendage to a life in which a house and two daughters came first. No matter what he tried, he couldn't win: if he wasn't boring his wife, he was doing something wrong.

At first he had no idea how to handle the new family dynamic. His own mother had died when he was six. His father, who never remarried, sent him to an all-boys Jesuit boarding school. So Osborne wasn't sure what to expect from a wife. Then one evening, over drinks at a Knights of Columbus dinner, he stumbled onto a secret: *many men were married to women like Mary Lee.*

And what did they do? They fished—but for more than just fish. Boats and lakes, rivers and streams, sports shops and bait shacks, led to banter and fun and the simple pleasures of time spent with good friends. As the years went by, the pleasant hours Osborne shared with his fishing buddies made up for what he missed in his marriage. And the few men he knew who fished with their wives? Those were men he envied.

But he had another reason for his affection for Mason. She was the grandchild who most resembled him. Whereas Cody and Beth were fair-skinned, blond and blue-eyed, Mason was the one whose skin tanned as dark as his. Her eyes were as black-brown and her hair as sleek and black as his had been at that age. Like her grandfather, she had inherited the cheekbones and the high, wide forehead that hinted of the Métis heritage. She might be a rascal—but he loved her.

"GRANDPA!" SHOUTED CODY as his bobber plunged.

"Set the hook!" said Osborne, jumping to his feet.

Water splashed and a grandfather nearly fell out of a rowboat, but a little boy reeled with all his might until a bluegill swung over the boat, sunlight shimmering silver off its scales. The fish was barely a keeper but the expression on Cody's face gave it the dimensions of a prized mount. Osborne removed the hook and slipped the fish onto a stringer. He handed the carton of worms over to Cody. "Okay, young man, your turn to bait the hook."

"But isn't that fish kinda small, Grandpa?" said Mason from her perch in the kayak. Osborne put a finger to his lips. "Oh," she mouthed, getting the message. She watched her brother fumble a worm, then said, "You know, I bet I can hook a hundred worms an hour."

"It isn't the numbers that count, Mason," said Osborne. "Fishing is all about quality, not quantity." Seeing the confusion on her face, he reminded himself that nine-year-olds are new to philosophy. "So what is this 'secret treasure' you found?" he said, doing his best to change the subject.

Before she could answer, they heard shouting from the dock. It was a woman dressed in police khaki (as opposed to the khaki that she wore in the trout stream)—the woman whose smile always sparked a wildness in Osborne's heart. Only she was not smiling now.

FIVE

"Cut the crap, Chuck—I do *not* have time for this…"

Cell phone pressed hard against her right ear, Lewellyn Ferris paced Osborne's dock, listening. Twice she tried to interrupt, only to nod with impatience. Using her free hand, she raked back the mass of dark brown curls that crowded her forehead. Osborne recognized the gesture: she was preparing to do battle.

As the rowboat glided toward the dock, he could see defiance in her dark eyes, tension in her shoulders. He let the boat drift as he watched, concerned.

He knew her as a woman slow to anger, a woman whose eyes smiled easily and whose manner was friendly—though that equanimity masked strength. But equanimity appeared to be in short supply at the moment. Did her adversary understand what he was up against?

Lew Ferris was not typical of many middle-aged women that Osborne knew, and the sight of her in her police uniform never failed to remind him of that. Of medium height, she had a figure that was sturdy and fit, breasts that were high and firm—evidence of upper-body strength. Where his late wife had been one to need help with a sack of groceries, Lew Ferris could be counted on to help you carry sections of your dock. Or take down a healthy twenty-two-year-old male who'd been over-served. Or, he was pleased to admit, change your life if she took off her shirt.

"No, Chuck," said Lew, her voice vibrating with anger. She was facing away from Osborne as she spoke. "No, no—*you* listen to *me*. I cannot keep five people waiting at the scene of a drowning accident—not to mention the ambulance crew and the victim who remains pinned under the boat—because your guys need a lunch break. Tell 'em to eat in the damn car!

"No—I cannot. I just told you I'm down to one officer on patrol because I have Todd assigned to the crime scene… Give me a break, Chuck—*there is no question it is a crime scene*." By now Osborne knew it was only the presence of his grandchildren that was keeping her from using stronger language.

She listened for a long moment, then said, "You know, Chuck, I don't know how it is in Wausau, but here in Loon Lake it is peak tourist season. We've got people trespassing on private land, fender benders in grocery store parking lots and altercations at boat launches—not to mention underage kids sneaking into bars.

"And, Chuck, that is *half* my day. But it is exactly why—if you don't get at least one of your men up here within the hour—I will file a complaint with Madison… Oh, you think I'm kidding? Try me."

The rowboat bumped the dock, causing Lew to turn. She rolled her eyes at Osborne. And with good reason.

While the Wausau Crime Lab was funded by neighboring counties and mandated to serve small townships like Loon Lake, its director, Chuck Meyer, had a problem: women. He did not believe they belonged in law enforcement and he never missed an opportunity to let Lew Ferris know it. Every time she called with a request for investigative assistance, he went out of his way to swamp her with bureaucratic baloney.

But what Meyer didn't know and Osborne did was that on most occasions Lew had the guy's number. She had refined a reverse psychology—not unlike that used on two-year-olds—that worked to finesse the jerk. Not today. From the expression on her face, Osborne could see she just wasn't going to take the time.

"No, Chuck, late afternoon does *not* work. Didn't you hear what I said? I've got *two* fatalities of which one is a homicide and my coroner can't be reached... He's on vacation—"

Whatever the comment that followed, Lew's face reddened under its summer tan. Her eyes flashed with anger. Throwing both hands into the air, she nearly dropped the cell phone before clutching it to say, "Chuck, goddammit. You tell me the last time I reported a homicide and was wrong. You *know* better than that. Now I want someone up here by one o'clock at the latest... Yes, I'll have the town attorney approve the expense. We've already talked—"

Again she listened, this time nodding, her face relaxing. Meyer must be backing off. As Osborne waited, he heard her say, voice calmer now, "Just one crime scene, Chuck. The other is a drowning up on the Tomahawk chain. From the sound of it, some girl got drunk and fell overboard. I can deputize Dr. Osborne to help me on that one. But I—"

She paused, shoulders straightening as she turned

toward Osborne—this time with a half smile and a wink. "Yes, Chuck, I'll have Marlene fax down the paper-work. Don't I always?" Again a brief pause before she said, "Okay, that works. I'll deal with the drowning victim, then meet your men at 2241 Loomis Road at one-thirty. Marlene has directions if they need them… Good. Thank you."

Clicking off her cell phone, she threw her head back, closed her eyes and gave a low, long groan before saying, "Dear Lord, why me?"

"So—having fun with the Wausau boys?" said Os-borne, getting to his feet in the boat, hands on his hips. "That's guaranteed to ruin a good day. Sounds like you have to cancel our fishing tonight." He didn't want to address the other subject until he could figure out a way to handle her disappointment.

"Don't know yet. Have to see how the afternoon goes. But, Doc, I am so glad I found you. Pecore is off playing his accordion at some damn polka festival and you heard the news—I've got two fatalities on my hands."

She gave Cody a look of apology as she said, "Hey, little fella, sorry to cut your fishing short, but I am in desperate need of a deputy coroner and your grandpa's the best I know. I'll trade you a carton of night crawl-ers if you'll let me borrow him—like, right away?" She smiled at Cody then shifted her gaze to Osborne. "I see Erin and Mallory are up at the house—maybe they can take over with the kids?"

Osborne hesitated before answering.

ANY OTHER DAY, he would jump at the opportunity—so pleased to work beside Lew that he had to make a conscious effort not to appear too happy around death. Half a dozen times since the night they met in a trout stream, he had been able to fill in for the coroner she despised.

Several facts conspired to make that possible. First, the Loon Lake coroner was appointed—not hired, not elected. A pathologist of questionable skills, Pecore held the position thanks to genetic good fortune—he was closely related to the wife of Loon Lake's mayor. And while she couldn't fire him, Lew did not hide that she was fed up with his incompetence, not to mention his binge drinking and a habit of allowing his golden retriever too near the autopsy table—all of which worked in Osborne's favor.

As often as she could find an excuse, the fly-fishing instructor—whom he had expected to be a man named Lou but turned out to be a police chief who spelled her name L-E-W—deputized Osborne.

He, in turn, had a new appreciation for his training in dental forensics, a developing science that he was exposed to during a brief stint in the military following dental school. Since meeting Lew, his interest in the field had escalated. That, plus his love for his profession, led to a decision to remain active in the Wisconsin State Dental Society. Just weeks ago he had attended a seminar on the latest developments in dental forensics—now termed odontology.

And since the Wausau Crime Lab had no full-time odontologist on staff, the potential for Osborne to be useful balanced nicely with the resulting opportunity to share a boat or wade a stream following a day's work with the Loon Lake chief of police.

"GOLLY, LEW, I WISH I could, but I promised Cody we would spend the afternoon fishing. It's his birthday." Osborne shifted his gaze from Lew to the worried eyes of the six-year-old sitting across from him. Cody had looked forward to the day for weeks and Osborne had set aside the entire morning and afternoon to be with him. Even their egg-salad sandwiches remained to be eaten.

Lew threw her hands up in exasperation. "Why does everything have to happen at once? But I understand, Doc, and don't worry—I'll figure something out. I'll call Crandon. They have a part-timer who may be able to help me."

She turned to jog back up the walkway toward his house, which was on the hill overlooking the dock. Osborne watched her go. Much as he wanted to help, he was torn—how do you break a promise to a grandchild?

Lew wasn't halfway up to the house when the roar of an outboard filled the air.

SIX

THE BOAT WAS AIMED straight for Osborne's dock. Seventy feet away, it made a sweeping turn to the left, throwing a wide wake. The driver cut the engine to let the bass boat bob sideways, bouncing over the wake toward shore.

Leaning back in a padded swivel chair bolted to a casting platform was a familiar figure in khaki shorts and a white T-shirt, his bare arms and long legs tanned dark by the summer sun. Cupping his hands to his mouth, the man in the boat let go with a distinctive trill.

"Cardinal!" shouted Cody, leaping to his feet so fast he nearly fell out of the boat. "I win, Mason!" he shouted to his sister. "I said so first."

THE KIDS HAD A RUNNING competition to guess what bird Osborne's neighbor might be imitating. They had six to choose from: four variations on loon calls, a robin on a sunny day and the cardinal. Ray was good enough that Osborne's early-morning coffee buddies at McDonald's now referred to him as "that human iPod with wings."

WATCHING RAY UNFOLD his six-foot-six-inch frame from the chair to plant both feet on the floor of the bass boat then gradually stand up—a process that seemed to take minutes—inspired Osborne to whisper to his grandson, "Cody, you know what I think? That guy's got more sections than a dragonfly."

Cody didn't hear. He was too busy pulling up the stringer to show off his bluegill. "Hey, Ray, look what *I* caught!"

"Whoa!" said Ray, the boat close enough now that you could see the angry olive-green muskie—flat snout gaping to expose killer teeth—that adorned the front of his T-shirt. Under the big fish ran the mantra: *Fish With Ray: Excitement, Romance, and Live Bait.*

"Cody, you razzbonya, you," said Ray with a whoop. "I better watch out or you'll have my job."

The little guy grinned so wide he showed every space where a tooth was missing.

Less happy was his grandfather, who had one thought: Not if I can help it.

RAY PRADT HAD A LIFE many men would covet. Spring, summer and fall he spent mornings and evenings guiding fishermen to his secret haunts of walleye and muskie, smallmouth, crappie and bluegills. Wind shouting through pines, sunlight shimmering on waves, a lonely loon calling with its heart—such were the blessings of Ray's good days.

The risk was weather—unpredictable in the northwoods and too often a disaster for business. Hot, humid days forced fish to lay low, disappointing clients and minimizing tips, while a blustery streak of rain and forty-five-degree temps would drive folks from the cities indoors.

To make ends meet, Ray cobbled together a mix of

odd jobs that ranged from digging graves for St. Mary's Cemetery to shoveling snow for the Loon Lake National Bank and shooting photos of deer, wolves and game birds for a local insurance company's calendar. Or, as he liked to boast, "Don't ever accuse me of a full-time job!"

Not a lifestyle Osborne would choose for his grandson.

It wasn't as if Ray couldn't have had a more traditional career. Well educated, he was the youngest child of a prominent Loon Lake couple. His father had been a respected physician. His sister was a successful lawyer in Chicago and his brother a hand surgeon. Ray was the one who dropped out of college to hunt and fish.

His critics would admit that as a fishing guide he excelled—but that was less a career than an excuse to avoid heavy lifting (though Osborne wasn't entirely convinced). What they dismissed were Ray's hidden virtues: he met few people he didn't like (and vice versa), he was a superb cook and he had perfected an endless supply of jokes—more than a few the far side of tasteful. Yep, his neighbor possessed all the talent and charm of a con man.

And Osborne excelled as his target. But as often as Ray might talk him out of his car or his boat or enlist him to help with difficult clients, Osborne didn't mind. He could put up with being conned, so long as it meant a stringer of bluegills or two fat walleyes left at the back door in recompense.

The fact was, he owed Ray for pulling him through long, dark nights. Rarely did he glimpse that head of rich, dark brown curls—always freshly shampooed and paired with the full, equally curly, reddish-amber (but laced with gray) beard—without instant recall of the first of the long nights.

That was the night of the blizzard when Mary Lee's lingering bronchitis turned deadly. In spite of snow drifting four to five feet deep and a windchill of fifty below, Ray had bolted on his plow to get them to the hospital, and drove the dangerous roads for a woman who had done her best to get local zoning officials to condemn his trailer and force him off his property—all because his beat-up mobile home compromised the vista from her living room window.

Mary Lee's demands were turned down, but that didn't stop her—she never missed an opportunity to badger Ray with angry comments and dark looks. Remembering those days now, Osborne had to smile. If Mary Lee only knew that the man she confronted so angrily so often was the same man who did his best to save her life. She would be apoplectic!

That night was followed by others—nights when Ray would follow him from bar to bar, making sure he didn't drive, ready to offer a ride home. While Osborne may have been unappreciated by his wife, she had framed his daily life. Without her there to order and organize, he was lost. So alone, it was easy to slide into booze.

His six o'clock cocktail became his four o'clock cocktail became the drink he had at noon. Soon all hours floated by. Ray, having been there himself, watched and waited for the day—or was it the night?—when he could persuade Osborne it was time for new friends. Ray's best friends—the ones who met behind the door with the coffeepot etched on the window.

And if *that* was a con job, Osborne was forever grateful.

"So, CODY, WHERE the heck did you hook that blue-gill?" said Ray.

Cody giggled as he shook his head. "I'll never tell."

"Right on!" said Ray. "You the man, Cody. You win the prize!"

"He does not," said Mason, paddling her kayak toward the bass boat. "That's a *little* fish—"

"Mason, honey," said Ray, "you miss the point. Your brother just proved he knows the cardinal rule of fishing—never, ever tell anyone where you caught your trophy. Smart guy, Cody."

"Yep," said Cody with pride, "we're all smart in our family. It's in the pants."

Ray tipped his head, puzzled. "In the pants? That sounds like one of my jokes—only I forget the punch line." He threw a questioning look at Osborne who shrugged, also puzzled.

"That's a first—you never forget a punch line, Ray," said Lew, who had hurried back down to the dock. "And how many times do some of us wish you had." She smiled down at Cody and said, "I think he means it's in their genes."

"That's what I said," said Cody.

"O-o-h, now I get it," said Ray. He gave Lew a look of surprise. "What's up, Chief? Playing hooky from the day job?"

"You'll be sorry you asked," said Lew as she walked out onto the dock. "I've got two fatalities and Pecore's off playing in a polka band somewhere. Doc can't help because he promised to take Cody fishing, but that doesn't change the fact I've got a homicide and a drowning on my hands. And I'm r-e-e-al short on manpower. If I need a deputy later today, are you available?"

Now Osborne felt even worse. For Lew to consider Ray as a deputy meant only one thing: she was desperate. Ray's penchant for poaching on private water and his occasional inhaling of the wrong kind of cigarette were not fully offset by the fact he was one of the best trackers in the region. Not to mention that he knew almost every Loon Lake resident, from lowlife to bank president. And if he didn't know someone, he would know someone who did. But hiring Ray meant having to hide his misdemeanor file.

"I think we can work something out," said Ray. "After I sauté that great catch of Cody's for lunch."

"Oh, really, really, Ray, would you do that?" Cody jumped up and down.

"Careful," said his grandfather, steadying the boat.

"Sure—but you only have one fish there, kid," said Ray. "Where's mine?"

Cody turned a questioning eye to his grandfather. Before Osborne could say anything, Ray gave him a wink and said, "Guess I'll have to go catch a few more—like some for me and Mason maybe, huh?"

"Can I go with you?" said Cody. Then he stopped and looked at Osborne with a guilty expression. "I guess not."

"Well, let's think about that," said Osborne. "Cody— would you like to fish with Ray? And I'll give Chief Ferris a hand?"

Osborne knew the answer before he asked. He was just a grandfather; Ray was a legend among young boys: an endless source of dumb jokes; a peerless chef whose shore lunch included ice cream bars; the man known to have caught seventeen muskies in one summer. Who would you rather spend a day with?

"If it's okay with the old man, Cody, you and Mason can ride in my boat with this new outboard I just bought. Take us maybe half an hour to catch enough fish for lunch."

"I'll run up and ask Mom," said Mason, paddling fast toward shore.

"Hold on, Mason. I'll check with your mom," said Osborne.

"O-o-h, this is the best birthday ever," said Cody, shaking both fists with excitement. Fishing with Ray put him in the big leagues.

"Y'know, Ray, that outboard looks familiar," said Lew, leaning to get a better look at the big, black outboard motor. "Isn't that the one that was in the accident last week?"

"Yep," said Ray, with a cheerful nod.

"You're kidding," said Osborne, giving the eighty-horsepower outboard a quick scan. The accident in question was one in which a teenager driving his father's boat after dark had run over two women swimming off their pontoon, killing them instantly.

"Got a great deal on it," Ray said. "Every tragedy leads to a discount, doncha know."

SEVEN

CROWDING INTO OSBORNE'S KITCHEN were all the important women in his life (at least those over the age of thirty).

First was dark-haired Mallory whose face always caught him off guard. The older she got the more she looked like the photo he had of his father's mother—same laughing eyes, same fresh smile. Then Erin, two years younger than her sister, as tall and slim as she had been at eighteen and still wearing her hair in a long, wheat-blond braid. And entering the room before him, as he hoped she always would: Lewellyn Ferris.

The slam of the screen door behind Osborne caused Mallory and Erin to look up from where they were hovering over a familiar figure seated at the kitchen table: Sharon Donovan. But this wasn't the Sharon Donovan that Osborne knew. The woman he knew had a laugh that burbled and rose-red cheeks dimpled with good humor. Not this morning—the Donovan perkiness was nowhere in sight.

"Oh my God, Dad, did you hear what happened to Nora Loomis?" said Mallory. "Any idea what…who…"

"No," said Lew, "we're waiting for the Wausau Crime Lab to give us a hand. We should know more later today. But I need your father—" She paused to stare at Sharon.

"Sharon?" Her voice was sharp with worry as she

leaned across the kitchen table to lay a hand on the woman's hunched shoulder. "You do not look good. Are you sure you're feeling okay?"

Sharon struggled to smile. "I'm better than I was an hour ago." She half rose to push her chair back from the table. "I'll get to work on your items right now, Dr. Osborne…"

"No, no, Sharon," said Osborne, motioning for her to sit back down. "This eBay thing is all the girls' idea so you three take your time. Erin, I—"

"Dad, before I forget, let me ask you something," said Erin, who had been listening with a preoccupied look on her face. "Did you know Mother had *twenty-five* place settings of china? I mean, what did she do with that many plates and saucers and soup bowls and coffee cups? For heaven's sake." The look on Erin's face was one of disbelief.

"Sweetheart, your mother wanted a black-tie life. Unfortunately," said Osborne, with a raise of his eyebrows and a shrug of apology as he turned to hang his fishing vest on a hook near the kitchen door, "she got me."

"I think she was a little out-of-date," said Mallory, her voice soft. She had been Mary Lee's favorite and her co-conspirator. Only since her mother's death had she and Osborne begun to find their way toward a kinship that should have happened years ago.

"So *you* don't want the china?" said Osborne, giving his eldest daughter a sharp look.

WITH HER MARRIAGE to the son of a prominent Chicago family—a management consultant boasting an MBA from Harvard—Mallory had come closest to fulfilling her mother's dreams. Until the perfect husband ran off with her best friend and Mallory flirted with a family tradition: alcoholism.

But the last eighteen months had been good ones for Mallory. Now she joked that she had to work to keep from getting her acronyms mixed up: she was about to complete an MBA in marketing from Northwestern while continuing to attend AA (and renew her membership in AAA).

"C'mon, Dad, never in my lifetime will I see a need for twenty-five place settings of china. That would be outrageous." Mallory tipped her head with a teasing half smile as she said, "Does that surprise you?" The message was clear: she was no clone of her mother.

"Maybe…just a little," said Osborne, meeting her eyes. Her answer made him feel good.

"Doc," said Lew, her tone urgent, "can you three discuss this later? Girls—" she raised her hands in apology "—no offense, but…"

"Gosh, no, get going," said Erin as Osborne grabbed his wallet from the kitchen counter with one hand while patting his shirt pocket with the other to be sure he had his glasses.

"Erin, what I started to say a minute ago is that Lew is deputizing me to help out for the next few days."

"I can see that, Dad. Not a problem."

"Yes, well, Pecore's on vacation and you heard from Sharon what happened at the Loomis place. Now I just talked to Ray. He's down on the dock with the kids getting ready to take them fishing and then fix lunch—"

"Dad, they'll be thrilled. Now will you get outta here!"

"And could you please take care of Mike for me?"

"Not to worry," said Erin. "I'll put Mason in charge of the dog." She grinned at Mallory. "Told you that SBF of yours would show up, didn't I?" Mallory blushed.

Osborne gave her a quizzical look but the impatience on Lew's face prompted him to drop any thought of asking a question. Stepping into the den, he reached for his instrument bag and turned to follow Lew out the back door.

"Drive with you or follow in my car?" he said as Lew hurried across the driveway ahead of him.

"Stay with me," she said, jumping into the police cruiser. "Faster this way. We'll stop by the Loomis house first—get your signature on the coroner's report so the Wausau boys are cleared to do their work."

"Lew, what's an SBF?" said Osborne as he buckled the seat belt.

"I have no idea." Nor, from the tone of her voice, did she care. "Doc, was Nora Loomis ever a patient of yours?"

"Yes, for years—both Nora and her late husband. Nice people. Not the kind who make enemies, Lew. I would assume she interrupted a robbery—don't you?"

"Possibly, but…well, I think it would be a good idea for you to do the official identification of the body."

"But Sharon knew Nora. Isn't that enough?"

Lew was quiet as she turned the corner off Loon Lake Drive to the highway. "You'll see what I mean…."

OSBORNE COULD NOT RECALL ever seeing so much blood. It had soaked through the cushions of an upholstered armchair near the body, splattered across the wall and a sofa, and pooled on the hardwood floor where Nora Loomis lay on her right side, left leg splayed back and shoeless. Bending over, he slipped one gloved palm under the left arm to feel the armpit.

"She's warm," he said, turning his head so Lew, kneeling beside him, could hear. "Hard to say if that's because of the summer heat or…it could be she's been dead only a few hours." He brushed back a bloodied hank of hair to expose lacerations and puncture wounds crisscrossing the woman's face. Lew was right: it was difficult to tell who this had been.

"Vicious, isn't it, Doc?" said Lew in a low tone. "Someone wanted to make a point."

Osborne nodded, continuing to study the still form and the patterns left by the weapon. "Looks to me like the carotid artery was cut," he said. "Could have been intentional."

"So she bled to death?"

"Tough to say." Scrutinizing the victim's head and neck, Osborne was reluctant to move the body and alter any trace evidence. He pointed to where flesh had been ripped away, exposing the upper left jaw. "I see part of a fixed bridge I made for Nora shortly before I retired—I'll confirm that from my records if Wausau needs the documentation. You can let me know after they do the autopsy."

"Any other observations? I'm having a hard time visualizing how all this happened," said Lew.

"Well…whatever the weapon was, it appears to have pierced the skull and very likely more than once. Blood is toxic to the brain, so that could also be the cause of death."

A wave of sadness washed through his heart, causing Osborne to drop his head in silent prayer, a blessing. Nora had been a kind woman, an easy patient who was always gracious and who paid her bill before leaving his office. He couldn't imagine how she, of all people, could be the target of such hate.

He extended his gloved fingers and, with a delicate touch, did his best to close her eyes—a gesture of respect to counter the horror. As if she knew what he was thinking, Lew patted his arm. Sitting back on his heels as he pulled off the gloves, Osborne shook his head. "Astonishing. The violence…"

"I know what you mean. I've never seen anything like it. Any guess as to what type of weapon was used? Those look to me like puncture wounds…"

Osborne straightened up. He had seen torn, ragged wounds like this once before in his life, a memory so ugly he hated that it came to mind.

TWENTY YEARS EARLIER, during deer season, one of the men in Osborne's hunting shack brought along a friend from out of town. Late on the second day of the season, the newcomer wounded a deer that took off across a swamp. Osborne offered to help track the animal, but the man insisted on retrieving something from his car first. Even though it wasn't his deer, Osborne refused to wait. He waded into the swamp, anxious to put the animal out of its misery.

But just as he found the deer, the newcomer showed up—with a weapon that he swung at the wounded animal. Osborne couldn't believe what he was seeing and rushed forward to fire his rifle. He killed the deer but he should have killed the newcomer. With one swing, the man had slashed across the deer just as someone had slashed at Nora.

"WHAT DO YOU THINK they used?" said Lew, staring down at Nora's body as she repeated the question.

"I'm not sure," said Osborne. "I have an idea but I hope to hell I'm wrong." Lew raised worried eyes to his and waited. "I saw someone use one of those old muskie gaffs once," said Osborne. "It tore through flesh just like this."

EIGHT

"MOCCASIN LAKE NEXT," said Lew, her face somber as they climbed back into the police cruiser. "Now you know why I'm having a bad morning." Osborne nodded. The sight of Nora Loomis hadn't made his day, either.

Moccasin Lake, located in the northwest corner of Loon Lake Township, was a good thirty-mile drive from the Loomis home. As they headed north, Osborne watched a cold front move in, the sky flattening to a dull gray as a west wind picked up.

By the time they reached the public landing where Marlene had arranged for the game warden to meet them in his boat, Osborne estimated the wind was gusting thirty to forty miles an hour and the temperature had dropped twenty degrees. The lake was whitecapped and the warden's boat was bouncing off the side of the pier.

"Hey, Pete, thanks for rearranging your schedule to help me out here," said Lew, bracing herself against the warden's extended arm as she climbed down into the heaving boat. "I take it you've been up to the site of the drowning?"

"Oh yeah," said Pete, shouting over the wind.

"Pete, Doc—you two know each other?"

"Oh yeah," Pete hollered. Osborne raised a hand in agreement.

Few were the fishermen who did not know Pete Rou-bideaux—fewer yet were those happy to see him. Rou-bideaux had a long, narrow face permanently dusted with a five o'clock shadow and tanned as dark as the darkest of the waters he policed. And police he did with vigor.

Osborne's coffee buddies kept a tally of Pete's scores on the bulletin board at McDonald's. Not a man among them had been able to avoid at least one uncomfortable encounter with Pete. The warden had an uncanny ability to lurk within (his) sight of your dock on that one morn-ing you risked casting just once, maybe twice, before purchasing your annual fishing license; or to pull up to your boat that one day that you were having such good luck you were sure you could sneak home with one walleye over the limit.

"Wolf Eyes" is what Ray Pradt took to calling Pete the day he got his third fine of the season (and it was only June!). The nickname mutated into "Wolfie" and stuck, though no one dared call him that to his face. Osborne, wobbling his way to a seat in the boat, made a mental note: do not slip up. The guy's name is Pete. Not Wolfie. Pete. Pete, Pete, Pete.

"Oh yeah," Pete shouted as he waited for Lew and Osborne to get settled, "nervous bunch up there. They were going to pull that body out from under that big pontoon of theirs but I warned 'em. Told 'em they'd be in big trouble if they touched a thing before law enforce-ment arrived."

"You're kidding," Lew shouted back.

"No, I'm not. Took a little convincing but I straightened 'em out."

Pete gave a sly smile and Osborne sensed he had exchanged more than a few words with the Moriarty clan that morning. "So, Chief, I went ahead and sent the ambulance crew up Birch Road and down a logging lane that'll get 'em kinda close to the channel. Ain't easy getting a vehicle in back there. Told 'em I'd come and get 'em when you're ready to move the body."

"Do we know who the victim is?" said Lew.

"Nope, but I know the family owns that boat. Moriarty. Outta Chicago—Lake Forest if I remember right. And you better believe those people got pull. I know from a buddy of mine works for the cops over in Minocqua that the old man's got that kid off speeding tickets and DUI's so many times…"

Pete shook his head in disgust. "Y'know that channel where they're stuck is right up from Party Cove. I'll betcha I give thirty tickets a weekend to drunks and some of the other razzbonyas who park their boats along there. Tell you what I *really* don't like? The ones that think the lake is their outhouse. I see 'em do that just once and they get a ticket for indecent exposure.

"Just so you know—that Moriarty pontoon has been up and down the cove almost every weekend lately. Real party animals those boys. Bad enough when you got an open deck, but those commodes get themselves a cabin they can hide in. I've been waitin' for something like this to happen. J-u-u-u-st waitin'."

Pete shook his head as he pulled the cord on his outboard. "One more thing," he said, sitting down as the motor purred and the boat turned into the waves. "It's too damn bad I can't give tickets to young ladies whose swimsuits are barely there."

Lew and Osborne exchanged glances: Pete hadn't missed a thing.

FROM A DISTANCE, there was no doubt that the two men silhouetted on the channel bank across from the stranded pontoon were related: same height, same hunch to the shoulders. But as the warden's boat drew closer, Osborne could see differences.

Bert Moriarty carried at least fifty more pounds than his son—a substantial portion of which belonged to a belly that hung over his belt with an authority gained from years of red meat and single-malt Scotch straight up. And while the older Moriarty was dressed for business in tan slacks, a green-and-white striped shirt open at the collar and a dark green sport coat, his son wore baggy black shorts, a purple T-shirt and a black baseball cap worn backward over a frizzy ponytail.

A speedboat—its hull a pristine white, banded with two stripes of nautical blue—was beached near the men, which explained how one of them had gotten there. Anyone trying to access the channel other than by water would have to use the logging lanes to the west and be willing to take a short hike across a swamp. The senior Moriarty looked too dry to have taken that route and too formal to have been lounging on the pontoon.

As the warden's boat rounded a final bend, Osborne got an unobstructed view of the stranded pontoon. Unfortunately, it was close to the eastern bank, which was bordered with a bog sure to hide deep pockets of muck too dangerous to wade. "How on earth are we going to move that thing?" he said. "And the wind—it's *pounding* that boat."

Pete cut the motor to let his boat drift close to shore. "Man, oh man," he said, "that sucker hasn't moved a foot since I was here half an hour ago. I was hoping the wind would shake that thing loose. Hey, Doc, you better pull us in so I don't wreck this prop."

Osborne waited for a pause between gusts before jumping out to drag the boat up onto the sand.

"Took you long enough," said a voice from behind him. Bert Moriarty strode across the grassy bank toward Osborne, hands in his pants pockets and an expression on his short, square, ruddy face that made it clear he had more important business elsewhere. Reaching to shake Osborne's hand, he said, "Chief Ferris, I'm Bert Moriarty and this is my son, Robert." The man spoke in blunt, clipped phrases.

"I'm not Chief Ferris," said Osborne, returning the handshake and trying not to stare at the man's expensive comb-over, which was standing straight up in the wind. "Dr. Paul Osborne, deputy coroner." Something about the guy's manner so irritated Osborne that he couldn't resist responding with the low, authoritative tone he reserved for people who doubted his diagnosis of gum disease—the ones who refused to believe that, untreated, all their teeth would fall out.

Bert glanced over at Pete, whom he appeared to recognize, then let his eyes settle on Lew. He walked to the boat where, hands on his hips, he did not offer a helping hand but stood watching her climb out before saying, "Mrs. Ferris, I am trusting you to deal with this situation in a *speedy* manner." Again, the flat staccato of a man used to giving orders.

"*Chief* Ferris," said Lew, her voice as brisk as his. "Mr. Moriarty, this *situation*—as you call it—involves a fatality. That means I will take all the time that's required to assess what happened here. And before we proceed, I want to make it clear that I do not appreciate the manner in which you spoke to my staff on the phone this morning. Profanity was *not* necessary. Now you two fellows get ready to help us move that big boat of yours."

"Oh, now…Chief Ferris," said Bert, "for heaven's sake. You can understand the emotional pressure this has put on my family. But you're right—" he raised his hands in a gesture of concession as he spoke "—I do apologize for anything I may have said under duress. Now I'm afraid—" he checked his watch "—my plane leaves in forty-five minutes. I'll give you the particulars and Robbie here can handle the rest in terms of the accident report and anything else you may need. My lawyer—"

"Well, Bert," said Lew, "I'll give you a choice. You can stand here and patronize me or, given that we have a victim caught under that boat, help *move* the boat so Dr. Osborne can get started on the coroner's report. Because no one goes anywhere until that happens."

Bert's mouth opened but before he could speak, Lew said, "State law."

They all turned to stare at the boat, which was only twenty feet away but across twenty feet of rough water. The customized pontoon was outfitted with a small cabin designed to look like an old-fashioned tugboat. Osborne didn't like the idea that the wave action might mean the underside of the boat was pounding away on a human body. The whitecaps made it impossible to see past the surface.

Bert must have guessed what he was thinking because he said, "Before the wind came up, Robbie was able to tell that the boat is hung up on a submerged log. He couldn't make out exactly where the body is but I'm sure it's under those logs, not under the boat. That boat's not…not…hurting anything."

"Mr. Moriarty," said Lew, her tone easy but firm, "much as your lawyer would like to hear that, you can't be sure. It's impossible to see what is or is not under the boat."

"But Robbie checked—"

"Dad, I didn't really—"

"Robbie, let me handle this." Bert's voice rose.

"Gentlemen," said Lew with a sweep of her arm that took in all four of the men, "we need to move that pontoon. How deep is this channel, Pete? Can we walk it?"

"Isn't that what we have tow trucks for?" said Bert.

"A tow truck," said Pete from where he sat in his boat, a smirk on his face. "How do you plan to get a tow truck in here—by barge?"

"Well…" Bert looked around and the reality of the landscape dawned on him. "Don't you have like…big fireboats to do this?"

"A boat the size of yours should not even be in this channel," said Pete.

"It drifted during the night," said Robbie, arms crossed over his chest and shoulders drooping. "I didn't mean to come up here. But, um, just so you know, there's kind of a deep drop-off in the middle, but you can cross up there where it's only like three feet deep." He pointed to a spot north of the pontoon.

"Okay," said Lew, "we'll cross there and work each end of the boat until we have it dislodged from whatever it's hung up on. Doc, you and I will take the end closest to the victim. It won't be easy with this wind but once it's loose—if the five of us can get to one side and push— it should float. Then, if you gentlemen will help Pete hold on to the pontoon, Doc and I will move the victim."

"Okay, Robbie," said Bert, stepping back, "you get in there and help out."

"Sorry, Bert, but with this wind, I need *both* of you helping out," said Lew. She turned and pointed to the pontoon. "I want Pete and your son at that end, Doc and I here and you in the middle."

Osborne and Pete moved to empty pockets, take off shoes and roll up pant legs. Lew, after removing the belt that held her holstered gun and the case for her cell phone, did the same. Robbie kicked off his flip-flops and walked down to the water's edge.

Bert hung back, watching, then said, "No, you can manage without me. I have a flight to catch and a meeting the minute my plane lands." Looking down at his wingtips, he said, "That's why I'm dressed like this."

"Bert," said Lew, standing at the water's edge with her hands on her hips and the wind whipping her hair across her face, "you strike me as a man who owns more than one pair of pants. Now, if you don't want to spend your entire day here, take your shoes off, roll up those cuffs and give us a hand."

Osborne had to turn away. Pete didn't—he had a big grin on his face.

The waves pummeled their backs and the channel's sandy bottom gave way too easily. But the water was warmer than the air, so it felt good—though Osborne hadn't expected to be wet up to his collarbone. As they took their places around the bucking pontoon, Robbie slipped and went under. He came up coughing.

"Goddammit," said his father, giving the boy's T-shirt a yank so hard the neck seam tore away.

"Jeez, Dad," said Robbie, "this is my favorite shirt. Take it easy, will ya?"

It took all five shoving hard against the wind, the waves and the boat before the pontoon slid forward with a muffled groan. The move released the victim.

The slender body of a female in tight, spandex flow-ered shorts and a lime-green halter top bobbed in the waves facedown. One on each side, Lew and Osborne guided the victim across the channel. The woman's skin was white and cold to the touch, colder than the water.

"That doesn't look like damage from the boat to me," said Lew as they struggled to slide the body up onto a grassy knoll. She pointed to where the hair plastered to the skull had been swept aside by the waves to expose gouges peppering the back of the head. "Those are not blunt force injuries."

In the meantime, Pete and the Moriartys had dragged the pontoon up against the west bank and out of the wind. Sliding and pushing, they managed to get the boat up onto the bank where Bert and Robbie helped Pete tie it to two pine trees. They finished just as Osborne was pulling his instrument bag from the warden's boat.

Walking over to where the victim lay on one side, her face turned away, he set down the instrument bag and reached in for two pairs of nitrile gloves. He offered one to Lew. Then, with hands gloved and gentle, they rolled the girl onto her back.

"Oh, God," cried Robbie, from where he stood watching over Osborne's shoulder. "Dad, it's DeeDee!" The boy dropped to his knees, staring at the girl. Then he stood and, hands over his face, staggered into the brush, vomiting. Bert slumped back against the beached pontoon, his jaw slack, his ruddy features turned gray as the sky.

"Bert? Robbie?" said Lew, looking around at the two men. "I take it you know who this is?"

"Yes, she's a friend of my son's," said Bert. "DeeDee Kurlander."

OSBORNE COULDN'T TAKE HIS EYES off the girl's head. Battered and swollen, her face was colored a very bad blue. As if she'd been the target of a scavenging eagle, the life had been dug from her eyes. But it was the trauma to the rest of her face and head that was, thanks to the cleansing water, startling in its detail: lacerating puncture wounds, bruises, even incisions. Her mouth hung open wide enough for Osborne to see that two teeth were missing—and not the work of a dentist.

Yet the body appeared to have been brutalized only from the shoulders up. With the exception of several yellow, translucent abrasions along her legs that may have been caused by the boat, the girl's torso bore no apparent signs of assault. Nor, aside from the deathly blue of her face, was there any postmortem lividity, the pooling of blood after death, which he found odd.

But it wasn't until Lew's fingers tightened around his elbow and her eyes caught his that it dawned on him what they were looking at: wounds inflicted by a cane-like weapon that could tear flesh; a weapon much too similar to that used on Nora Loomis.

IT SEEMED AN HOUR but it was only minutes before Lew stood to say, "Pete, would you please send the ambulance crew back to town? I'll need the Wausau boys here before we move the victim or that pontoon. Please—Bert, Robbie—don't anyone go on board that boat for any reason until the crime lab has finished its work.

"And, Bert, this is no accident. You'll need to cancel your flight."

The man nodded. Gone was any air of condescension. Bert Moriarty looked scared.

NINE

"MAN, THAT IS A BODY built for sin."

"Carrie! Shut up! Why do you say that?"

"*You* shut up, Juliana. Chief Ferris asked about DeeDee and guys—and I'm repeating exactly what I heard 'em say every time she showed up in her bikini. And you know darn well DeeDee didn't mind—she took it as a compliment."

Legs crossed, her right foot pumping with vigor, Carrie added, "They meant it in a nice way."

DeeDee's two roommates, their mascara smeared from tears, were answering Lew's questions from where they sat, one on each side of Marcy Kurlander, mother of their late friend. To Osborne's eye, the tableau of the three women offered quite a contrast in female decor and demeanor.

BOTH GIRLS WERE TALL, exceedingly slender and dressed in long tight jeans, spike heels and sleeveless tops so short they barely covered their midriffs. Aside from the soft smudges of mascara along their lower lashes, they were so well made up and their hair so carefully coiffed—one blond, the other a blond/brunette hybrid—that they looked more like models in a magazine than flesh-and-blood young women. Osborne wondered if DeeDee had worn life with the same gloss.

Unlike the polished twentysomethings who sat with their arms around her, Marcy was a woman whose face had fallen, leaving her with skin the texture of tissue paper and minuscule lines fanning down from the corners of her eyes. As if an afterthought, her short, flat brown hair was shoved behind her ears; and for make-up she wore only a swipe of rose-pink lipstick that did more to showcase the vertical lines above her top lip than she might have intended.

Since Marcy, on hearing from the chief of Loon Lake Police, had rushed from her office to the rental house DeeDee shared with her two best friends, she was still in the boxy green scrubs required for the head nurse of Loon Lake's assisted-living facility. The uniform did nothing to compliment her squared-off figure, which was likely the result of too many hours spent in a chair filling out insurance forms.

But however disheveled she may have seemed at first, her faded-but-honest prettiness coupled with the quiver of despair in her voice evoked, for Osborne, a grace lacking in the two girls.

"So LIKE I SAW DEEDEE right around eleven o'clock last night and she seemed perfectly fine," said Carrie.

"And where was this exactly?" said Lew, jotting down the details.

"The parking lot for the public landing at Moccasin Lake. But like I said, she was fine."

"No one else around? No one she was with?"

"No…not right then…"

"How about you, Juliana?"

"I saw her last as she left the pontoon to go with Carrie."

"And that was the Moriarty's pontoon, correct?"

"Yes," said both girls simultaneously.

"Okay," said Lew, "let's back up a bit. Dr. Osborne and I need you to give us some background on Dee-Dee—her other friends, her job, who she was dating, any problems she was having…"

Getting the girls to talk was not difficult. Shocked at the news of their friend's death, the roommates spilled over with details and kept interrupting each other as they outlined DeeDee's eccentricities, her daily routines, the boys she knew, her attitude toward her boss and colleagues. The DeeDee they knew was a girl whose days, nights and weekends revolved around clothes, makeup, power bars, low-calorie shakes, flavored martinis, guys and parties—a life just like their own.

As the young women spoke of their friend with eyes wide, backs straight and hands flashing to emphasize their words, Marcy sat silent, her back tense against the sofa cushions. As she listened, her face reflected mute incomprehension—part grief, part astonishment—at what she was learning about her daughter.

"WAS THERE ANYTHING DeeDee might have done to put her at risk?" said Lew, when the girls paused long enough for her to get a word in.

"Well…" Carrie lingered, thinking, then shrugged as she said, "Y'know, when it came to calories, she wasn't logical. Like, she worked out every day but then she would play beer pong. You know—in a couple hours drink over a thousand calories worth of beer? Go figure."

"Carrie! Not like you don't do it, too," said Juliana.

"Yeah, well, we're talking about DeeDee here, not

me. Plus—" Carrie pouted "—I don't work out every day. It's not the same."

"Beer pong?" said Osborne. "I take it this is some kind of game?"

"Oh, Doc—you haven't heard about beer pong?" said Lew. "The bars hold tournaments sponsored by the distributors and it's become quite a problem for law enforcement—way too much beer drunk in a short period of time. The players get hammered.

"You girls correct me if I'm wrong, but as I understand the game, one team stands at one end of a table in front of a triangle of Dixie cups half-full of beer and pitches ping-pong balls across the table into the opposing team's cups. When a player sinks a ball, the other team's player has to chug the beer and remove the cup from the table. The side that runs out of cups loses— but who cares if you're overserved when you're having fun. Right?"

"Yeah, that's how we play it," said Carrie with a sheepish half grin.

"So was DeeDee a contestant, or just an observer?" asked Osborne, hoping for Marcy's sake that it be the latter.

"Oh, she was great," said Carrie. "In the coed contests, she was our team champ!"

"Jeez, Carrie, put a lid on it, will you?" said Juliana. The mother hen of the three, she was, unlike Carrie, keeping a close eye on Marcy's reactions to everything being said.

It HAD BEEN ALMOST two-thirty before Lew and Osborne had been able to grab a bite of lunch, then stop back out at Osborne's so he could pick up his car. Then back in a rush to the rental house where DeeDee had been living. When they arrived, Marcy Kurlander and Carrie Koronski, the receptionist for a Rhinelander dermatologist, were waiting for them. Juliana Stevenson, the third roommate, was on her way from the school where she taught kindergarten.

Lew had been hesitant to interview the three women together but Marcy had argued persuasively that it would save time. Not only could she add to what the girls knew but she wanted answers to the same questions: who had last seen DeeDee and where? But as the girls talked, Osborne realized that Marcy had not been that close to her daughter. In fact, the more she heard, the more desperate the swoon in her eyes.

"Oh...WHAT DID I SAY WRONG?" Carrie's voice trembled with uncertainty. It seemed to be dawning on her that beer pong was sounding less fun and less hip by the moment.

"Should we assume that DeeDee, like everyone else on a team, could get pretty hammered at times?" Lew kept her tone light, encouraging.

"I hate that word," said Marcy, muttering under her breath.

Carrie clamped her lips shut and avoided looking at Juliana.

"Carrie," said Lew, "we're not looking to blame DeeDee for playing beer pong. We need to know if and how she may have put herself at risk. I can see you know more..."

"Okay, okay," said Carrie with a wince. "DeeDee had this thing she liked to do before heading out. Have a couple beers to get a pre-game buzz going—get in the mood, y'know?"

"Whoa—now that is just enough! I am sorry, but I do not believe a word of what's being said here," said Marcy. "I know damn well my daughter was not a drunk, Chief Ferris. She had a hell of a lot more on the ball than—" She caught herself before she could say, "Carrie." Instead, she said, "Than…than…drinking games. I can swear…" She waved a finger to make a point but choked up.

"Mrs. Kurlander's right," said Juliana, jumping in. "DeeDee was very hardworking. They loved her at her job—"

Osborne could feel the interview spinning out of control. Lew must have, too, because she raised a finger to quiet Juliana, then said in a voice that was calm and measured, the low tone of the confessional, "Marcy, our children are never who we think they are.

"I've been where you are right now. My son was knifed in a bar fight and it wasn't until his funeral that I learned from his friends how much he had been drinking. To this day, as a parent, I wonder how it was that *I* didn't know. But we don't, we can't—because we raise them to live their own lives, we *have* to let go, we have to let them make their own mistakes."

Osborne resisted the urge to speak. He wanted to curb Marcy's despair from his own oblique angle. He wanted to add to Lew's words: Nor are *we* who they think *we* are. Look at me—I'm in AA. I was such a good parent that my oldest child is in AA. We all live with dumb mistakes—the ones we make, the ones we cause, the ones committed by people we love. But he said nothing.

"Well…" said Marcy with a tremor in her voice. "I know very little about what the girls have been saying here but I guess…I suppose some of what they say is true. DeeDee is always so upbeat that it makes sense she loves to party, and I know she tries really hard to keep her weight down. What girl her age doesn't? I had no idea about the drinking but that's her business. She's twenty-two years old after all. I mean…she *was*…twenty-two." Juliana rubbed Marcy's shoulders as she spoke.

With a surge of resolve, Marcy pushed herself up to lean forward on her elbows. She clasped her hands in a tight ball, dropped them between her parted knees and gave them a determined shake before looking hard at Lew and Osborne. "Okay, we know she partied, we know she drank, but that's not the whole story. If you're going to find the person who did this, you need to know more and let me tell you my DeeDee had *plans*…"

Marcy couldn't finish. She pressed the fingers of one hand against her eyelids as if she thought she could stop the tears running down her cheeks. Their own eyes brimming again, DeeDee's friends folded their arms around her.

"Carrie shouldn't have said so much," said Juliana with a heavy sigh.

"But Chief Ferris said the smallest detail might be important," said Carrie, glaring at her friend over Marcy's collapsed shoulders. "I'm not *trying* to hurt anyone's feelings."

SOMBER, PATIENT, LEW AND OSBORNE remained seated in worn armchairs across from the women. Osborne gazed around the living room of the rental house, which was small but tidy and decorated with used furniture. A vase of fresh daisies sat on a beat-up coffee table that also held fashion magazines, a scattering of CDs and DVDs, a bottle of silver-blue nail polish and an iPod plugged into its charger. Outside an open window, a honeybee buzzed.

Once Osborne had secured the information needed for the death certificate—age, last birthday, legal residence, cause of death (TBD)—he had, at Lew's request, taken the chair next to her. She introduced him as the acting coroner and a deputy who would be assisting in the investigation. Osborne was always surprised at how pleased he was when that happened, even though it had been nearly two years now that she had come to rely on his participation and perspective in difficult interrogations.

Years in the dental office spent listening for the mundane detail that might clarify the source of a patient's problem had given him an acute ear. Was that pattern of wear due to poor orthodontics? Or was the patient under severe emotional stress? Add to that the reality that men and women hear things differently—not to mention vary their responses when quizzed by a member of the opposite sex.

And so it was that Lew and Osborne had learned to count on surprising each other when they compared notes.

MARCY REACHED FOR the Kleenex box on the coffee table. As she leaned forward, Juliana shot a look at Carrie. Osborne caught the exchange and knew what it meant: Carrie had just been ordered to say nothing that could cause Marcy more distress.

The older woman blew her nose, then raised her head and said, "Do you know that when her dad died of a heart attack two years ago, DeeDee offered to help me pay the mortgage on my house? I mean, *that* is the kind of person she was. And did you notice her closet—how well organized she is…was…"

Marcy was right. A quick survey of DeeDee's bedroom while waiting for Juliana to arrive had shown she was orderly in her habits. The closet door—ajar as if DeeDee had left in haste—exposed a hanging rack with each item of clothing on its own hanger and hung with like items: slacks with slacks, blouses with blouses, jackets with jackets. Above the rack was a shelf loaded with shoe boxes. An inside wall of the closet held more shelving on which were arranged dozens of pairs of shoes. Organized against one wall of the small bedroom were more sandals, heels and tennis shoes—each shoe paired with its mate.

"She had a passion for stilettos," said Carrie at the expressions of amazement on the faces of Osborne and Lew. "She loved buying online and always found the best deals. She was a perfect size six so she could do that, y'know?"

"Doc," said Lew, turning to Osborne, "DeeDee wasn't wearing shoes, was she?"

"No."

"Do you think you could identify her shoes if we were to find them?" said Lew to Carrie.

"Probably. Lately she's been wearing Campers—the right foot is different from the left so they're pretty distinctive. I'd recognize any of those for sure."

The top of an old oak dresser and a bedside table held

gaily colored cardboard boxes brimming over with bracelets, earrings and other items of jewelry. On the floor beside the bed, which had been made with a lemon-yellow coverlet and matching pillow, was one empty water bottle and a half-eaten power bar tucked neatly into its wrapper. The drawers to DeeDee's dresser and the nearby desk were closed.

"Don't you want to see what's in her desk?" said Marcy as Lew turned to leave the room.

"Not yet," said Lew. "Without a search warrant I can only examine what is in plain sight, which is why it is very important that no one touch anything in here until I examine all her belongings. I should have the search warrant by dinnertime, I hope."

"But you don't need a warrant," said Marcy. "The girls and I don't care. We want you to do everything you can."

"I appreciate that," said Lew, "but it's a legal issue that protects any evidence that's found. A formality, but critical in a courtroom."

"Do you want us to close the door?" said Carrie.

"Yes—oh, wait," said Lew, pausing in front of the dresser on which a mirror framed in oak was set. Wedged along the bottom edge where the mirror met the frame were three trout flies—feathered lemon yellow and tipped with a spray of deer hair. "These trout flies," said Lew, pointing, "beautifully tied Conehead Madonnas. You don't see those very often. Did DeeDee fly-fish?"

"Oh, heavens no," said Marcy. "My dad made those. He was a fly fisherman and loved to tie trout flies. Dad adored DeeDee—he called her 'my little Madonna' and made those for her when she was just a little tyke. I think Dad was kidding when he said he needed strands of her blond hair to make them perfect—but DeeDee believed him."

Marcy loosened one trout fly from the mirror. "Maybe…I'd like to bury one with her. Dad would have liked that…" She took a deep breath, then paused. "Oh, dear, I'm disturbing things right after you said—"

"No, please, take it," said Lew, raising a hand to keep Marcy from putting the trout fly back in place. "I'll make a note. So long as no one touched anything more in this room, that will be fine."

TEN

"So, Marcy, you were saying that DeeDee had plans," said Lew when the woman had regained her composure. "What kind of plans?"

"Her career," said Marcy, taking a deep breath. "She's been working at the Chamber of Commerce for almost a year now. Loved the job. Two weeks ago, they gave her a nice raise and a promotion. We had dinner together last Sunday and she told me she planned to go to school part-time for an associate degree in business and public relations. The Chamber sponsors a program that allows you to do that at the tech college over in Rhinelander."

"That's what she told me, too," said Juliana. "Her boss said she could have Fridays off for school."

"So…no problems at work?" said Lew.

"Hardly," said Juliana. "They had like eleven applicants for the new business liaison job and DeeDee got it. Her annual review was excellent—they told her she was a natural. Like these job fairs she's been doing? She got so many people to come, it was like unreal."

"Juliana's right," said Marcy. "DeeDee felt so lucky when she got that job—it was fun, she made decent money and it came with an SUV even—used, but a nice car. I know she was putting in at least eight hours a day."

"More!" said Carrie, eager to deliver good news for a change. "Golly, Mrs. Kurlander, I know days she worked ten, twelve hours. Partly 'cause she would drive to the locations to make sure everything got set up right."

Lew checked her watch. "Doc," she said, "it's not quite four-thirty. I'm scheduled to meet with the Moriartys and their lawyer at six. If I have Marlene call the Chamber and ask those folks to stay a few minutes, would you mind stopping by and asking them a few questions?"

"Fine with me," said Osborne. "It's obvious I have to change any plans I had for later this evening, so please, Chief, use me where you can." He gave her a regretful grin as he spoke.

"I'm sorry, Doc," said Lew, her apologetic glance acknowledging his reference to their aborted plan to spend the evening in a trout stream. She reached for her cell phone, saying, "I haven't even had a chance to talk to Nora Loomis's son yet and Marlene's logged two calls from him, poor man. Girls, anyone in particular at the Chamber that Dr. Osborne should contact? Who was her immediate boss?"

"Anita Rasmussen," said Juliana, "but maybe that Mr. Curry, too. He thought she was doing great work. He said he'd write her a recommendation for school if she needed it."

"Yeah, you better talk to him all right," said Carrie. "He was starting to hang on DeeDee. I found him sitting in his car watching our house one night last week—"

"Carrie! You know he had files for DeeDee. He wasn't lurking," said Juliana. "Just because you didn't like him doesn't mean anything." Carrie shrugged, her lips tight.

"Good," said Lew as she reached Marlene and left the two names along with the instruction to call back only if the Chamber people couldn't see Osborne.

"Something else," said Carrie, after Lew had completed her call. She shot a defiant glare at Juliana, then glanced around to be sure everyone was listening. "Mr. Curry paid her a *very* nice bonus."

"What do you mean by 'very nice'?" said Marcy, turning on the girl. "Are you implying that DeeDee was—"

"Oh, gosh no," said Carrie. "It was a real bonus. Ask Mr. Curry. He told her his job fairs had never had such terrific turnouts. But, jeez, an envelope with two hundred dollars in it? DeeDee was pretty taken aback."

"That is a nice bonus," said Lew. "A very nice bonus."

"Ye-e-a-h," said Carrie, "but DeeDee wanted to give it back. That's what she told me, anyway."

"Did she give it back?" said Lew.

"I dunno," said Carrie.

"I'm sure she did," said Juliana.

"So she was working for the Chamber *and* for Mr. Curry?" said Lew. "Did she have *two* jobs?"

"No, no," said Juliana with a shake of her head. "Carrie is confusing you. The Chamber offers new businesses in town the services of their liaison team for a limited time. Mr. Curry was planning to hold six job fairs in the region and DeeDee was assigned to help with three—one in Rhinelander, one in Loon Lake and the last one was this past week in Minocqua."

"Speaking of Minocqua," said Lew, "how well do you girls know Robert Moriarty?"

Quizzical expressions crossed both girls' faces, then

Carrie said, "Oh! You mean Robbie? I've never heard him called Robert." She giggled. "*Robert?* That's funny. I can't imagine him as a 'Robert.' Sounds so serious."

"So you know him well?"

"Oh sure, we party with Robbie all the time. Like I said earlier—we were all on his boat last night. DeeDee, too, of course."

"Right…" said Lew. "So tell me more about Robbie. Were he and DeeDee a couple?" The girls looked stymied. Neither one spoke.

Osborne decided to change the subject. "So you said that the last you saw your friend was around eleven last night in the parking lot at the public landing on Moccasin Lake Road."

"That's right," said Carrie. "But that was after we left Robbie's boat—and the party."

"And where was the boat at that time?"

"Where it always is—the north end of Party Cove just past the public landing. Is…is that the boat where…?" Carrie's eyes widened with disbelief.

"Yes," said Lew, "only not at that location. Robbie said his boat drifted up the channel by mistake. Were you aware of the boat drifting when you were on board?"

"No," said Carrie. "Except for when they brought us back to the landing, it was definitely anchored."

"Are you saying Robbie didn't mention that DeeDee was at the party?" said Juliana, her surprise genuine.

"He hasn't had an opportunity," said Lew. "His father insists their lawyer be present when his son is questioned. Carrie, why don't you fill us in on exactly where you and DeeDee were last night—the entire evening, not just the last time you saw her."

Carrie plucked at something on the knee of her close-fitting jeans. "Oh…well, yeah, Robbie had a big party last night and we were all there. DeeDee went straight from work 'cause she worked late, so she was already on the boat when I got there."

"Was this one of your beer pong parties?" said Osborne.

"Oh, no, just friends—it was Robbie's birthday. He invited a bunch of us. And then…" Carrie paused, concern in her eyes as she struggled to recall the events the night before. Osborne wondered if she had had so much to drink that she couldn't remember clearly.

"Juliana, I take it you were there?" said Osborne.

"Yes, but I stayed on board when Carrie left with Jeremy and DeeDee."

"Yeah, then this weird thing happened," said Carrie. "Well, no, maybe it wasn't weird—forget what I just said."

"Wait a minute. Carrie, if you're holding back for my sake," said Marcy, "don't! Chief Ferris needs to know everything, anything. Me, too." Marcy put an affectionate hand on Carrie's knee. "I promise I am not going to be angry with you…please."

"It's not that," said Carrie. "It's just…I'm trying to figure this out…"

"Let Dr. Osborne and me figure it out," said Lew. "You give us the details and we'll take it from there."

"Here's the thing—it was weird that DeeDee left us the way she did. See, we ran out of beer so me, DeeDee and Jeremy decided to drive to the filling station up on Highway 47 for another case. But when we got to the landing, DeeDee changed her mind and said she would wait for us in her car because she had to make a phone call.

"We were gone maybe fifteen minutes at the most

and when we got back she wasn't there. Her car was but she wasn't. I figured she was back on the boat, but I realize now she wasn't. Thing is," said Carrie, a stricken look on her face, "I didn't pay attention, not even when we were back on the boat. I just assumed she was hanging out with somebody."

"Because why?" said Lew. "You were otherwise engaged?"

Carried turned red. "Kinda."

"What kind of phone call?" said Marcy, oblivious to Carrie's embarrassment. "She had a cell phone, why wouldn't she have stayed with you and made that call?"

Carrie's eyes darted to Juliana, then away. "I dunno. I just assumed it was a private call."

"Do you know who she was calling?" said Lew.

"No," said Carrie. She answered so quickly Osborne knew she was lying.

"Well, enough for now," said Lew, standing up. "Marcy, I will be in touch with you as soon as the pathologist has completed the autopsy. If you're making arrangements…" Lew beckoned the woman into the corner of the living room where she spoke in a low whisper. Osborne heard enough to know she was advising against an open casket.

Marcy nodded, brushed away some tears, then struggled to speak. "So…we don't have any leads yet on who…"

"We may not for a while," said Lew, her voice gentle.

"Marcy," said Osborne, getting up to join the two older women, "I don't know if it helps to know this—but my preliminary exam indicated your daughter lost consciousness immediately."

Marcy inhaled deeply. "I hope so. But I will want to know…how…you know?"

"Of course you will," said Lew, patting her shoulder as they walked toward the doorway. "Oh, and, Marcy, I'll let you know when the team from the crime lab has finished with DeeDee's car. They're hoping to find trace evidence there that could give us a good lead. So I have no idea how soon they'll be releasing it."

"That's okay," said Marcy, "I understand."

ELEVEN

AFTER WALKING MARCY to her car and watching as she drove off, Lew turned to Osborne. "Poor woman. I know how she feels. You go home, you sit down, you look around, you feel absolutely cold inside and all you can think is, My child is dead. And if you're like me— unkind—you think, Why my child? Why not the meth addict kid of that worthless piece of shit down the road?"

"That's *unkind?*" said Osborne. "Sounds like an honest reaction to me—maybe the only way to deal with life's unfairness. I wouldn't blame anyone for thinking that way." He paused, expecting Lew to walk over to the police cruiser. But she stayed where she was, checking back through her notes. Anxious to get over to the offices where DeeDee had worked, he said, "Lew, ready to head out?"

"In a minute, Doc. I asked Juliana to step outside— alone. Would you mind waiting with me? Marlene would have called if you had to rush over to the Chamber. Oh, and, sorry about the fishing. I was looking forward to it."

They lingered on the sidewalk outside the girls' house, the late-afternoon sun hot on their shoulders. Osborne checked his watch. "Too warm for trout tonight anyhow, Lew. Don't feel bad."

"I could use the break, Doc. Let's see how it goes tomorrow. We're never in the river before eight anyway. It's just that tonight I have paperwork up the wazoo. And I have *got* to take time with the Loomis family."

"Nora's son, Russell, was a patient of mine all through high school," said Osborne. "Would he be offended if you had me talk to him after I meet with the Chamber staff?"

"That's a thought," said Lew. "I'll try to give him a call before I meet with the Moriartys. Marlene said he's driving in from Eau Claire late today. If he doesn't mind, that works for me. I'll leave a message with Marlene—and, Doc, you have to get yourself a cell phone. This is ridiculous."

"Lewellyn, I cannot get cell service at the house. Even Mallory's reception is spotty, and she has Sprint."

"Dr. Osborne, are we standing in front of your house?"

"No."

"Well then."

"Okay, I'll look into it but—" He was interrupted by the ringing of Lew's cell phone. With a wink, she pulled it from its case.

"It's Ray," she said, seeing the number in the digital display.

RAY WAS ALREADY ON THE JOB, having gotten a call from Lew shortly after capping off Cody and Mason's shore lunch with ice cream bars. Half an hour after that Lew was able to clear the one hazard she always faced when attempting to deputize the keenest eyes in the northwoods: a misdemeanor file that reflected a hankering for controlled substances and a dedication to fishing private water. It was the poaching that got the game wardens most upset. But Lew had her ways—not to mention an abiding affection for Ray that she did her best to hide.

While still at the site where they had landed the Moriarty boat and pulled the victim onto the bank of the channel, she had asked Pete not to leave until she could reach the Wausau Crime Lab to request more help—a request that was granted the minute Bert's name was mentioned. Apparently, his lawyer had already been on the line demanding an expert investigation versus "any of those Loon Lake bozos." That was just fine with Lewellyn Ferris.

However, still needing someone to guard the site and DeeDee's body, her next call was to Pete's supervisor, Ken Deitz, in the Department of Natural Resources offices. She got him on the first try. After listening to her request that he allow the game warden to guard the area and the corpse until the Wausau boys arrived, Ken had paused then said, "Sure, but on one condition, Chief—you gotta tell me where you caught that big brown you're holding in that photo on the bulletin board at Ralph's Sporting Goods."

"Come o-o-n, Ken," Lew said, "you are way out of line asking me that." Then, as if the entire Wisconsin Fly-Fishing Listserv was eavesdropping, she lowered her voice to say, "Check page twenty-two in the fishing regs—and don't tell anyone you heard it from me. Got it?" Ken chortled and approved as much of Pete's time as she might need.

And so she turned to Pete, saying, "Warden, I have one small favor to ask. I need you to keep your hands off one of my deputies for a while."

"And who might that be?" Pete said, rolling a tooth-pick between his teeth.

"Ray Pradt. I need eyes on the ground and he's the best—you know that as well as I do."

"A-w-w-h, Chief, do I have to? I make my quota on that guy."

"Two weeks—hands off. Then business as usual."

Pete nodded. "Unless I find him growing pot."

"Pete…" She saw his silly grin. "Stop pulling my leg, I am not in the mood."

"I'm not pulling your leg—but I'll ease up on the guy. Y'know, I keep thinking maybe one of these days he'll live by the rules…"

Lew caught Osborne's eye. Not likely.

Pete wasn't the only Loon Laker who questioned (or was it envied?) Ray's disregard for the emblems of re-sponsible adulthood: 401Ks, annual inspections of septic tanks, and health insurance. Or as an overserved patron at Marty's Bar said one night when Osborne and Ray stopped in to have a couple Cokes after a good night's fishing: "I can't believe it—a family like yours and you dig graves and go fishing every day? What the hell kinda life is that?"

Ray would just smile and shrug and answer the phone when his critics called for help after a dog or a child went missing in the woods, a fisherman did not return for dinner or a bird hunter stumbled on a peculiar set of bones that could be bear…or human?

Of course, if a woman badgered him, Ray gave her the romantic version: "I don't know, hon," he would say. "I've been this way since I was a kid. I'm addicted to wildness, y'know. Love the neighborhood—squirrels, chippies, eagles, deer, a couple turkeys, two loons, half a dozen woodpeckers, oh, and a bear just moved in."

After she swooned and offered to support him, Ray would decline with a gracious grin and say, "Thank you, sweetheart, but I am happy as I am. I may not have money in the bank but I got the sunset—all those colors! For free!"

What he also got for free was a ticket to the outdoors and a talent for tracking. Lew had no difficulty arguing that Ray was one of few people north of Chicago who could read sign on the ground, on a tree or in brush and know in an instant if it was the result of weather, creature or human interference. And so his talent trumped the misdemeanor file. Who knew you could be paid for seeing what others miss, for seeing what should be and isn't?

"THAT'S FINE, RAY," said Lew, cell phone pressed to her ear as she listened for a long minute from where she was standing on the sidewalk, one eye on the door to the rental house. "Not sure about Doc, but why don't you and I plan to meet at the Moccasin Lake public landing at eight-thirty tomorrow morning. I have a seven a.m. with both Wausau teams—the guys working the Loomis property and whomever they send to work the Moriarty boat. It'll be short, just an update on what they got so far. I'll head your way right afterward. I'd like a better look at the Moriarty boat—inside and out.

"But you're right about the channel—once it's dusk, don't push it. Oh, and on your way out tomorrow morning, would you mind stopping by the Loomis place? Todd assures me he walked the grounds inch by inch—

but I'd feel better with one more set of eyes. Wausau may be the best indoors but when it comes to wooded areas, those boys are way too coat and tie."

"Has he found anything?" said Osborne as Lew tucked her phone back into its case.

"Not yet. That asphalt parking lot didn't leave much to go on. After the crime lab moved DeeDee's car, Ray scoured the perimeter a good hundred feet into the brush and said he can find no signs of a struggle or of anyone going any farther than they might if they wanted to use the bushes instead of the restrooms. He's willing to bet our victim may have left—or was taken—in another vehicle."

"Given what we heard from the girls, whoever she talked to on her cell phone might know something," said Osborne.

"And if we can separate those two, we may find out just who that is," said Lew, crossing her arms as she leaned against Osborne's car, which was parked in front of her police cruiser. "I'm not leaving here until I have one more chat with Miss Juliana. She's our weak link."

"How do you figure that?" said Osborne.

"Because she cares. And she's not stupid."

"Ah." So he and Lew agreed, Carrie *was* the less bright of the two. "Where's Ray headed now—back here?"

"No, he said he tried taking his canoe up the channel against the current and it wasn't too bad. On the chance that our victim may have entered the water at a point north and drifted down toward the boat, he's going to give that west bank a good look up until dusk. What he doesn't cover today, he'll tackle first thing in the morning. Which is fine with me—tough tracking in the dark."

The front door of the rental house opened and Carrie

tripped down the stairs, swinging a small purse and waving as she said, "Chief Ferris, I'm meeting up with my folks—we're going to make sure Mrs. Kurlander gets something to eat and has help with stuff. She and my mom are good friends."

"Good, Carrie, you have my cell phone number if you remember anything," said Lew. "Is Juliana going with you?"

"She's meeting us at the Loon Lake Pub. Right now she's on the phone—I don't know who with 'cause it just rang."

"One more thing, Carrie," said Lew. "Sometime tomorrow you'll hear from another one of my deputies. I've asked him to do a complete search of the channel and the stream banks leading up from Moccasin Lake. I'm hoping we can determine the exact spot where DeeDee's body entered the water. Ray Pradt is his name."

"Oh, Ray—he is so cute," said Carrie. "Sure, whatever I can do to help."

"He won't be in the business of being cute," said Lew. "He's going to need specific details from both you and your friend Jeremy—where you were standing and walking when you last saw DeeDee and exact times."

"Oh, sure," said Carrie. Then, as if she had something else that she wanted to mention, she paused to study the pavement for a long moment before opening the door to her Honda Civic. Whatever it was, she decided to drop it and jumped into the driver's seat.

"Lew," said Osborne, checking his watch again, "I better leave if I'm going to get to those folks at the Chamber before it gets too late."

Just then Juliana flew toward them from the doorway

of the house. "Ohmygod, Chief Ferris, that was the bank that just called. DeeDee opened an account last Friday with a check for twenty thousand dollars—and all that money is missing! It was withdrawn early this morning."

"Calm down, Juliana," said Lew. "Which bank are you talking about?"

"First National. That was Bob Carlson, the president. He asked to talk to DeeDee so I told him what happened. That's when he told me she had opened the account but the money was withdrawn. He asked me if I knew what she might have done with the money. You want his number?"

"We'll have it at the office. Juliana, before Dr. Osborne and I leave, I have a question for you."

"Oh…" The girl's eyes darkened.

"Who do you think DeeDee was calling on her cell phone? Mr. Curry?"

"Oh, gosh no. Heavens, no. That guy gave her the creeps." She stalled.

"Juliana," said Lew, "look at me. This is a homicide case and if you withhold information, you become an accessory. Now DeeDee's dead and any promises you may have made died with her."

"I know that." Juliana hung her head, letting strands of streaked hair fall across her face to hide her eyes.

"Well?" Lew's voice was firm, uncompromising.

"She was sleeping with Robbie's dad," said Juliana, her voice low and deliberate, the cadence of a person aware that every word they say is changing someone's life. "Since May, I think. I didn't know till a couple weeks ago."

Juliana gave a heavy sigh as she raised her head to meet Lew's eyes. "DeeDee knew it was crazy but she was in love. And he's a rich guy, y'know? She said he promised they would get married."

TWELVE

OSBORNE HURRIED ALONG the pebbled sidewalk leading into the old mill building that had been converted into offices for the Loon Lake Chamber of Commerce. It was nearly five o'clock and he hoped he wasn't too late.

The front doors opened to a spacious reception area lined with racks holding maps and brochures. A doe and her fawn, so expertly mounted that Osborne half expected them to walk toward him, welcomed visitors. A human—not mounted—looked up from behind a desk as he entered.

The human was a tall, lanky college student whom Osborne recognized as the nephew of Dick Nelson, one of his McDonald's buddies and owner of the True Value Hardware store. "Dr. Osborne?"

"Hello, Ryan. I didn't know you worked here. Sorry to be late. Is Mrs. Rasmussen still in the office?"

"Oh yes, she's been waiting for you." The boy jumped to his feet. "If you'll follow me…" As they walked down a short hallway past a kitchen area and a restroom, he looked back to say, "I'm the summer intern."

"Oh," said Osborne, "I'll bet that beats unloading trucks at your uncle's store."

"You betcha," said the boy, with a shadow of a grin that disappeared as he added, "Y'know, Dr. Osborne, I still can't believe the news. I *didn't* believe it at first. Everyone here is so upset. DeeDee was so cool." Under the bright lights of the hallway, Osborne could see the boy's eyes were red and swollen. He had been crying.

They rounded a corner to enter a large open area that featured walls bare to the original brick; a ceiling open to HVAC ducts; a long room divided so that one side held workstations with computers and phones and the other a conference area defined with a dark green rug boasting the Loon Lake logo. Six chairs crowded around a pine table. Two of the chairs were occupied.

"Paul, sorry to see you under these circumstances," said Anita Rasmussen as she got to her feet. She was a tall, large-boned woman with short, blond hair streaked gray, a gray that matched her tailored pantsuit. Anita had run the Chamber for years and served on the St. Mary's school board with Osborne when they both had children in school. He knew her to be a careful, detail-driven manager. DeeDee's organizational skills would have appealed to Anita.

"I'd like you to meet Hugh Curry," said Anita, turning to a heavyset man squeezed into the chair beside her. "Hugh, this is Dr. Paul Osborne—he is the deputy coroner for the Loon Lake Police Department and assisting with the investigation of DeeDee's…um…death."

"Mr. Curry," said Osborne with a handshake, "I heard your name from DeeDee Kurlander's roommates. I understand she'd been assisting you as part of her responsibilities here at the Chamber?"

"That's correct," said Curry, pumping Osborne's hand. Anita nodded in agreement. Like Anita, Curry was dressed for business in dark slacks, a light blue sport coat and a red tie that Osborne couldn't help but notice held a large grease spot.

"These are sad and terrible circumstances," said Curry, holding tight to Osborne's hand. "She was a fine young woman and I just can't imagine how such an awful, awful thing could happen." In spite of his size, Curry had a thin, wheezy voice. He spoke slowly, enunciating each word as he continued to shake Osborne's hand. It wasn't until he had finished every word that Curry let go. Osborne was thankful he hadn't asked the guy to recite the Gettysburg Address.

Anita sat back down and Osborne took the chair next to her. She waved at Ryan, who was on his way out of the room. "Tell you what, Ryan—since you and DeeDee were such pals, why don't you sit in on this with us. Speak up if you think of anything you can add."

Though he seemed relieved to be included, the boy had a tense, worried look on his face. He pulled a chair out and sideways to make room for his long legs. After sitting down, he leaned forward, elbows on his knees, and proceeded to bounce one fist against the other— right against left, then left against right.

"I'm sorry," said Curry, twisting to face the boy, "would you stop that? You're driving me nuts." Anita shot Ryan a sympathetic look and nodded at him to do as requested.

Defiance flashed across Ryan's face and told Osborne everything he needed to know about the relationship between the boy and the older man. Offices, thought Osborne, as dysfunctional as families.

"I asked Hugh to make a special trip into town to meet with us," said Anita. "DeeDee has been working closely with his company to set up three of six job fairs over the last two months and I thought Hugh or some of his people might have some insights or information that could help the investigation. Hugh?"

"Gee, Anita, ever since you called I have racked my brain and I can't think of a thing," said Hugh, a tremor in his hand as he reached for his cup of coffee. He picked up the cup, noticed the shaking and set it down without taking a drink.

"I was hoping—did you check with your staff?" said Anita.

Curry ignored the question. "That young woman was just a super, super gal. Like I said before, I can't imagine… I mean—who on earth would do such a thing? I have to tell you the news sure came as a shock to me and to…" His voice trailed off.

"And to whom?" said Osborne, reminding himself to be sure to get the names and phone numbers of people working for Curry who would have known DeeDee.

"Well, my wife, of course. She worked closely with DeeDee. If I can say anything, I would like to repeat what I was telling Anita before you arrived—that girl was so diligent. She made sure all the rentals arrived on time, that everyone signed in correctly, that coffee and donuts were on hand…

"You know—" he turned to Anita "—I just thought of something. Could she have irritated one of our vendors?"

"That they would bludgeon her to death?" asked Anita, looking at him askance. "That's a stretch, Hugh." Her tone told Osborne everything he needed to know about Anita's opinion of the man. He was beginning to wonder if DeeDee was the only one who'd gotten along with the guy.

Osborne checked him over more closely. The man wasn't just heavyset, he was bordering on fat. His attempt to hide incipient jowls behind a well-trimmed mustache didn't work, nor could he hide the double chin—or the sweat beading across his forehead. And his skin was winter white—in the middle of July? He was one of those men that Ray would describe as "smells like indoors."

"Hugh," said Anita, tapping her ballpoint pen on the blank pad of paper on the table in front of her, "what about all those people attending the job fairs? You have applications from the participants that Dr. Osborne and Chief Ferris could use if they needed to reach any that might be of interest, correct?"

"Yes, I have that information but never, not once, did I see any inappropriate behavior during our events. I would discourage you going in that direction, Mrs. Rasmussen."

"But how can you be so sure?" said Osborne, interested in Anita's point. "A pretty, blond girl as outgoing and attractive as DeeDee would naturally attract more than a few men of her age—I would think." Even as he spoke, Osborne was thinking "men of any age." "I agree with Anita," he said. "We should look into the attendees.

"In fact," said Osborne, hitching his chair forward, "we could start by comparing any incoming phone calls that DeeDee may have received with phone numbers on those applications. That wouldn't take long. Then—"

A clacking across the wooden floor behind them caused Osborne to pause and glance back toward the reception area. Heading their way was an Idaho potato suspended on two toothpicks. At least that was Osborne's first impression—and one of which he was not proud.

Though she appeared to be of average size from the waist up, the woman boasted a horizontal expanse of derriere that was remarkable: high, wide and measuring more than a foot from front to back. Perhaps it was the black leggings and heeled sandals she was wearing that accentuated her rear end—not to mention the legs that appeared too thin to support all that weight. Or maybe it was the shirt: a close-fitting purple pullover with a V-neck exposing more cleavage than Osborne wished to see.

He concentrated on keeping his eyes glued to her face, which was definitely her best feature. Round and full-cheeked with flawless pale white skin and lips outlined in scarlet, she had the eyes of a chipmunk: black and tiny and gleaming with intelligence. Her hair was a shiny black bowl cut to the line of her jaw. If he made an effort not to look down, she reminded Osborne of a porcelain figurine from the Orient.

"Hello, everyone!" boomed the woman over the chatter of her heels. Her deep, cigarette-cured voice filled the long, high-ceilinged room. "Sorry I'm late—had to pick the dog up at the vet's."

"My wife, Gwen," said Curry, half rising to his feet, his voice a wheeze against his spouse's baritone.

"Hah—don't anyone dare stand," said Gwen with a bark intended to be a laugh. Though for what reason she would laugh, Osborne hadn't a clue.

Mrs. Curry plunked herself down next to her husband, set one hand over his and peered around the table before saying, "May I speak for Hugh and myself? As a family business, we are *devastated.* Poor, poor Dee-Dee. You have *got* to let us know what we can do. This is a tragedy. An absolute tragedy."

Osborne stared down at Gwen Curry's hand. Every finger, except her thumb, featured a ring. Each ring held a precious stone in an ornate setting—a diamond, an emerald, a garnet and maybe (Osborne wasn't positive) a sapphire? Gwen caught his eye and said, "Antique jewelry—I sell on eBay." An officious tone coupled with the arch of her right eyebrow implied retail success.

"My wife is a power seller," said Curry with pride. He gave Gwen a fond look. Anita looked at her, too, but with exasperation. This meeting was not about Gwen.

"*Platinum* power seller," said Gwen with another hoarse bark before Anita could speak. "There is a difference, you know."

"I—we weren't expecting you, Gwen," said Anita, frustration creeping into her voice. "So if you don't mind, we'll continue our discussion here. Hugh and I were updating Dr. Osborne on DeeDee's activities over the last few days—"

"Well…you want the truth?" The woman's eyes darted around the table to be sure everyone was listening.

"Of course," said Anita. "That's why we're here."

"That girl did her job just fine until a week ago when she let it all go to hell," said Gwen.

"Gwen, hold on now," said Hugh.

"*You* hold on," said Gwen. "That old saying, you don't speak ill of the dead—I don't believe in it. And these people should know the girl was a flirt out looking for a sugar daddy and things like this are *exactly* what happens when you're not careful."

Anita looked stunned.

Hugh stared down at the table. "I think that's a little too strong, Gwennie. She did a very, very good job for us—" A crafty look stole across his face. Osborne got the distinct impression that he was happy to shift blame toward his wife.

"You better believe she did," said Anita. "Your attendance for the job fairs that DeeDee worked was double what we expected—more than the tech college gets!"

"Until Hugh gave her that outrageous bonus and she stopped making the effort."

"Is that true, Hugh?" said Anita.

"I hate to say it, but Gwen's got a point. It did seem like once she had everything she needed from us, she dropped the ball. I didn't want to say anything because we were winding up our events here in northern Wisconsin, so what good would it do?"

"Yes, that's what I told Hugh—what good would it do?" said Gwen, a smug look on her face. "She would just make up some goddamn lame excuse."

"I'm sorry," said Osborne, anxious to defuse the situation. "I missed something here. Would you folks mind taking a minute to walk me through the basics? Exactly what does your firm do and how many people are on your staff?"

"Seven full-time employees, including Hugh," said Gwen.

"Just my wife and I," said Hugh.

Anita looked from one to the other. "Which is it?"

"Oh—hah," said Gwen with a bark, "you mean just

Hugh's operation? Running the Curry Job Fairs takes just the two of us. But me—I employ six people. Power selling requires manpower."

"Really," said Anita. "Mr. Curry, when you approached us in February, I distinctly recall you telling me you had a Minneapolis-based recruiting firm employing one hundred fifty people. Did that change?"

"Oh, that," said Curry. "You misunderstood. That's the franchise main office." He looked over at Osborne. "We hold job fairs all over the country and I own the upper Midwest franchise."

"I see." Anita tapped her pen. She caught Osborne's eye. She did not misunderstand; she was lied to.

Gwen glanced at her watch. "I have an auction in thirty minutes, people. If you don't mind, Hugh and I have to leave. Any more questions—just give us a call."

"Dr. Osborne, do you have any questions?" said Anita.

"Yes, I do, thank you, Anita. Hugh, I know Chief Ferris would appreciate copies of all the registrations, applications—whatever it is that people filled out at those job fairs. We can't eliminate anyone who may have spoken with DeeDee these past few weeks."

"Or had intercourse with her," said Gwen, muttering under her breath.

"Excuse me," said Anita, standing to tower over Gwen and making no effort to hide her anger, "that is enough. You are out of line, Mrs. Curry. Way out of line. I am ready for you to leave this office." She pointed toward the front entrance.

"All right, all right—I take it back," said Gwen, "but you didn't see what I saw."

"Well, I'm not interested in what you *think* you saw.

Now, Dr. Osborne has made a request that requires an answer." Anita was vibrating.

Still hoping to curb the tension, Osborne repeated his question to Hugh. "How soon can you get those to us?"

"If you mean the applications, that's a problem," said Gwen.

"Dr. Osborne didn't ask you, he asked your husband," said Anita.

"We're partners in the business," said Gwen, fixing her tiny eyes on Anita.

"I don't understand. What could be the problem?" said Osborne.

"We promise confidentiality to our attendees," said Hugh. "Tell you what, I'll give our lawyer a call and I'm sure I can get those to you in a few days."

"Tomorrow morning is when they're needed," said Osborne. "As early as possible. Chief Ferris will be in her office by seven."

"We'll see," said Gwen.

"Well, if I were you," said Osborne, in the tone he had perfected for use on obnoxious patients when recommending they seek the services of a dentist other than himself, "I wouldn't want to be accused of withholding information critical to a homicide investigation."

With a poutlike thrust of her chin, Gwen got to her feet, waited for her husband to fight his way out of his chair and took the lead leaving the room. As she walked away, Osborne was surprised to see that the seat of her leggings was white with dog hair. Or was it cat hair? Whichever, the woman was a mess.

When the front door had slammed behind them, Anita raised both hands, saying, "Oh, how I detest those people. They've been nothing but trouble for us all spring. DeeDee worked so hard to keep them happy. That woman—talk about *demanding*.

"And that man—do you know how many times I've driven past here late at night and seen him in this office with all the lights on? When I ask him why, he's very evasive. He lies—certainly lied to me about the size of his firm. Yes, sirree, that guy's up to something. It doesn't take twelve hours to print out the job fair handouts. Yuck." She shivered. "I can't wait to get those two out of here."

"I just hope they deliver those applications," said Osborne, feeling defeated. Gwen Curry had taken control of the session and he didn't like it.

"I'll call the DA this evening because those applications are the direct result of a Chamber initiative," said Anita. "We won't wait on those two. I doubt they even have a lawyer. What frauds! He really did tell me his firm employed one hundred fifty people. My fault." She shook her head. "I should've done a background check."

"DR. OSBORNE?" said Ryan as he and Osborne walked past the kitchen area toward the front door. "Do you have a minute?"

"Certainly," said Osborne. He didn't, but something in the boy's demeanor throughout the meeting gave the impression he was on the verge of saying something but kept deciding against it.

"In here," said Ryan, waving him into the kitchen and shutting the door behind them. Keeping his voice low, he said, "You need to know something—DeeDee was planning to file a sexual harassment suit against Mr.

Curry. She warned him early last week, the day before he gave her the bonus. When she got the envelope with all that money, she was sure he was trying to buy her off."

Speechless for a moment, Osborne pulled out a chair from the kitchen table and sat down. "Does Anita know this?"

"No. DeeDee had an appointment with an employment lawyer in Wausau next week. She wanted to handle things right before telling Mrs. Rasmussen. She didn't want to risk losing her job. Thing is, Mr. Curry was going to contract to run more job fairs and DeeDee couldn't stand the thought she might be assigned to work with him again."

"He was? The Currys told us they were 'winding up' the job fairs. You think they're planning more?"

"He told DeeDee he was. He wanted her to work full-time for him. See, I don't think Mrs. Curry knew because then he went into this whole riff about how he was tired of taking orders from her and maybe he and Dee-Dee could get together. Yada yada. DeeDee was totally creeped out."

"What kind of harassment are we talking about—do you know?"

"Oh, I know all right. She told me all about it."

WHEN RYAN FINISHED describing DeeDee's struggle to maintain her professionalism and deal with behavior that included inappropriate touching, lewd jokes and lurking outside her bedroom window in the dark, Osborne walked back toward the conference area, hoping to find Anita in her office, but she was gone. Leaving the building alongside Ryan, he noticed that his was the only car in the parking lot.

"Ryan, do you need a ride somewhere?"

"No, thank you, I have a bike. Got it from Uncle Dick. Hold on—" The boy jogged past a row of shrubs, ducked behind the shrubbery and emerged wheeling a small Japanese motorcycle. "Isn't this cool? I'm paying for it with the money I'm making here this summer. Uncle Dick got a deal from one of his suppliers."

Ryan reached for a helmet hanging over the handlebars and pulled it on.

"Looks like fun," said Osborne. "Just don't hit a deer on that thing. By the way, Ryan, don't be surprised if Chief Ferris will want to talk to you some more about the situation between Mr. Curry and DeeDee. In fact, I'm sure one of us will call you tomorrow. I also think you should tell Mrs. Rasmussen everything you told me. She doesn't need any more surprises."

"Not a problem. I want to help."

Osborne started toward his car. "Oh, one more question. Would you say DeeDee was upset when she left the office yesterday?"

"She's been upset since last week," said Ryan. "Yeah, real upset. But I think I'm the only person she talked to about it. She was angry but she was embarrassed, too. She said the whole thing was so cheesy and she asked me if I thought she did anything to bring it on, y'know."

"And what did you say?"

"I told her 'no.' Without question 'no.'"

"Ryan, did you and DeeDee date?"

"Oh, no. Gosh, no. We were really good friends but she was a couple years ahead of me in school. She went with older guys."

"Like Robbie Moriarty? Do you know Robbie?"

"Not really. He was a friend of DeeDee's but from what she said, just a friend. See, we talked a lot—DeeDee and me—but always just in the office. I don't really know all those people that she partied with. They're older, y'know."

"Did DeeDee ever come to work drunk?"

Ryan looked at Osborne with a shocked expression on his face. "DeeDee was so professional…" The boy's face twisted and he clenched his eyes shut for a few seconds, but he pulled himself together and said, "The DeeDee I knew was hardworking, pleasant, pretty—all those things. Never once this summer did I ever see or hear her do anything unprofessional. Anything. Did someone really tell you that?"

"No," said Osborne, "but I had to ask."

"Because if someone said that, I'll—"

"No one did, son. Believe me, that is not why I asked. Now I've kept you long enough, Ryan. You've been a big help."

"But late," said the boy as he slipped his key into the bike's ignition. "Way too late. I should've said something earlier." His cheeks were wet.

"Don't beat yourself up, kid," said Osborne, patting him on the shoulder. "No one saw this coming. No one."

THIRTEEN

OSBORNE HAD NO NEED TO CHECK with the switchboard for a message from Nora's family. Her son, Russell, was waiting in the conference room adjacent to Lew's office.

"He's been here for over an hour," whispered Laura, the young night dispatcher, to Osborne as he walked in. Laura was Marlene's twenty-two-year-old niece. Just starting a two-year associate degree in law enforcement, she had lobbied hard for the dispatcher job to see how a police department operated. Whatever she may have expected her duties to be, caring for a bereaved but handsome man her own age was not one of them. Laura's cheeks were flushed, her eyes wide with worry.

"I didn't know what to do or say when he came in," she said. "I got him a Coke—was that okay?"

"That was very considerate," said Osborne with an assuring pat on her shoulder. "Have we heard from Chief Ferris?" It was nearly seven. He hoped Lew might be on her way back from the meeting with the Moriartys and their lawyer.

"Not since she left," said Laura. "Been pretty quiet this evening. We had a 9-1-1 for a kid who took a softball in the face. The EMTs are on their way to the ballpark—but nothing else."

"Let's hope it stays quiet," said Osborne, heading down the hall to the conference room.

"Dr. Osborne," said Russell Loomis, standing up as Osborne entered. Sandy-haired and tall, Russell had the athletic build of a soccer player, which he had been in high school. Osborne knew him as a bright kid with a quick grin. No grin today—his features were slack with grief.

"Russ," said Osborne as they shook hands, "I don't know where to start, son. Chief Ferris asked me—" Before he could say more, he was interrupted.

"I went to the morgue. They won't let me see my mom."

"They can't. Not until the pathologist from the Wausau Crime Lab has finished the autopsy. Then you can, but, Russ, I'm not sure you should. I suggest you wait until the funeral home has an opportunity—"

"I know, I know. I used to date Carleen Kiel, one of the nurses over there, and she told me my mom was pretty beat up. I couldn't get her to say more." Russell fastened his gaze on Osborne. "What the hell happened, Doc?"

"We'll know more in the morning," said Osborne. "Right now all we can say with authority is that your mother's death was no accident. But as to exactly how she died and when—we have to wait for the autopsy results."

Russell looked away, then shook his head as he raised one hand in frustration and said, "You know, I've been feeling like something was going to happen. A premonition in the pit of my stomach. Even though it made my girlfriend madder 'n hell, I had this urge to see Mom so I drove home last weekend—I mean, it's only four hours from here to Minneapolis."

A sheepish look crossed his face as he said, "My mom always said she was kinda psychic and that I inherited that from her. We had a little agreement between us to pay attention to that kind of stuff. That's what made me decide at the last minute to drive over."

"Ah, so you were here in Loon Lake this past weekend?"

"Yeah. It seemed silly at first 'cause when I got here not a thing was wrong, in spite of this nagging feeling that she might have a health problem or something."

"She must have been happy to see you." Osborne didn't add what he was thinking: one of Nora's last thoughts might have been gratitude that she had been with her son so recently.

"Oh yeah. And fact is, the pontoon wasn't running right so I was able to fix that and a couple other things around the house. Little stuff, y'know." The boy's eyes reached for approval.

"You have to feel good about that, given what's happened."

"Well, yeah, that and the fact I was able to take her fishing." Russell's face lightened. "After I got the pontoon motor running, I took her up the river for smallies—just like she and Dad used to do on Sunday afternoons. And, Doc, would you believe she landed a seventeen-inch smallmouth? That son of a gun weighed over two pounds! I told Mom she should keep it and we'd get it mounted for the den but she insisted on releasing it. Whoa, that was one monster smallmouth—I know I've never seen one that big. And he fought—man, Mom loved it."

"What was she using?"

"Dad's favorite tackle—a Zoom four-inch Dead Ringer on his Carolina Rig." Russell's smile belied the haunted look in his eyes. "I am so glad I came. I am so glad she had such a great time with that fish…"

And then he wept. Osborne moved from his chair to sit alongside Russell and wait. Laura opened the door to check on them but Osborne waved her away. Then he did for Russell what Ray had done for him: he held his hand.

"SO THERE WAS NOTHING BOTHERING your mother," said Osborne when Russell had regained his composure.

"Oh, you know, she was stressed out over that job she started. She didn't need to work, you know. Dad left her well off but Mom has always been involved—she needed something to do and when she was offered one within a week of attending a job fair, she felt like it was meant to be."

"Well, Russ, think it over and call me at home if anything comes to mind. Here's my number at the house," said Osborne, getting to his feet. It had been a long day and if it was okay with Russell, he would just as soon talk with him again in the morning.

"I did come across one weird thing today," said Russell, getting to his feet, too. "I stopped by the bank where I've been helping Mom with Dad's estate. They said she opened an account with a check for twenty thousand dollars late last week—and that the money was withdrawn early this afternoon. Now, Dr. Osborne, that doesn't make sense, does it?"

"Certainly does not. Which bank is it?"

"Mid-Wisconsin."

"Really," said Osborne. "I'll alert Chief Ferris to that as soon as she's back in the office. Did they say how the withdrawal was made? Maybe your mother had arranged for bills to be paid automatically from her account."

"I think I would know if she had a bill for twenty thousand dollars. She would have mentioned it to me."

As they walked down the hall toward the doors that led to the parking lot, Russell said, "I just wish she hadn't let herself get so wound up over that dumb job at Universal Medical."

"What was it that bothered her? The long hours? Didn't like the people?"

"No, she liked the people all right. It was this one incident that threw her." They were in the parking lot approaching Russell's car when he said with a shrug, "But, you know, it's the kind of thing you have to expect from those call centers."

"What kind of thing are you talking about?" said Osborne, stopping to listen.

"Well, Mom was never in management before, so being a boss was a new dynamic for her. Part of her training to be a supervisor meant working the evening shift and taking calls for a couple of weeks so she would have a feel for the system. It was something that happened with one of the calls that worried her."

Osborne set aside his feeling of fatigue. "And what was that, Russ?"

"She said she overheard a drunk threatening to kill his wife. She told her boss and they said they would look into it, which they did up to a point, I guess. They told her they couldn't trace the call so there was nothing more they could do. Mom worried that the woman had been hurt—maybe killed. She was letting it keep her awake nights."

"When did this happen?"

"Early last week."

"You don't happen to know who she worked for out at Universal, do you?"

"A woman by the name of Fern Carstenson. In fact—" Wayne reached for his wallet "—I have my mom's new business card with their main number here."

"I'm going to check into this," said Osborne, shaking Russell's hand. "You do your best to get a good night's sleep. Are you sleeping at your mother's?"

"No, I'm staying with good friends—the Moores. You can reach me there or that nice girl on the switchboard has my cell phone number."

Back in the police department, Osborne hurried down the hall to the empty conference room. He reached for the phone console on the table. Fern Carstenson was due in for the late shift at 10:00 p.m. He left a voice mail asking her to call him at home.

FOURTEEN

HE DROVE HOME THROUGH ghosts. The morning cold front had collided with the humid afternoon sun to charge the night with a slithering, shape-shifting fog. Trees, barns, utility poles had turned grotesque—unrecognizable in the moonless air. Branches jutted at unnatural angles, mimicking the contorted limbs of dead women. Even the statuesque balsam guarding the corner where he turned off the highway had morphed into a threatening presence, hanging over the road with arms stretched out to strangle.

Peering through the fog streaming across his driveway, Osborne was relieved to see light beaming from the open kitchen windows. As he closed the car door he could hear Mallory talking to someone, her sentence ending in a peal of laughter followed by a hearty masculine chortle. Ray. Had to be, as there was no other car in the driveway.

"Dad? Hey, Dad, is that you?" His daughter peered through the screen over the kitchen sink. "Have you had anything to eat? Ray brought pizza—saved you some."

"In a minute," said Osborne with a wave she probably couldn't see. "Taking Mike down to the lake."

He reached for the flashlight stored on the shelf just inside the garage door, then opened the gate to let the dog out. Mike, leaping with joy, left a slather of love on Osborne's right hand. "Off!" he said without conviction. Sometimes unconditional love was not a bad thing.

Reaching the dock, he made sure to throw a stick so far it would take Mike minutes to retrieve. He smiled as the dog sailed into the cloud bank, confident of success, Mike was one air-scenting Lab who wouldn't let a little fog get in *his* way. The sound of Mike's slurping as he swam comforted Osborne. Unsettling as the day had been, it was good to know some things never changed. As he waited, listening to the waves play their notes along the shore, he let fatigue and the emotions of the day wash over him. Then he heard a snap of jaws and a swirl as the dog spun toward shore.

"DAD? DAD, YOU HAVE GOT to see this! Ray has a brilliant idea." Mallory, seated in front of the laptop computer that she had set up on the desk in the den, turned eager eyes to Osborne as he walked in. Ray was leaning over, one hand on her shoulder, studying the screen.

"Mind if I go for the pizza first?" said Osborne. Three years of Ray Pradt's brilliant ideas had taught him that a five-minute delay would not be catastrophic.

"Thanks again for helping out with the kids, Ray," he said, loud enough so he could be heard in the den. He shuffled through the kitchen cabinet in search of a paper plate and a napkin. Finding a plate but no napkin, he ripped off a section of paper towel. It dawned on him he was starving—he wasn't used to eating so late.

"Ohmygod, Dad, you should have seen Cody," said Mallory, bouncing into the kitchen as Osborne inhaled his first wedge of pizza. "Ray let him wear his hat—all through lunch. I took pictures. It was so cute."

"I'm sure," said Osborne, his mouth full. Once again, he couldn't compete.

RAY'S HAT WAS LEGENDARY: a stuffed trout sewn onto a battered leather cap so that the head and tail waved in the air over all six feet six inches of its proud owner. In the summertime, the cap's earflaps were tucked up into the crown, allowing Ray to tip the trout "just so." And "just so" required time and effort. The McDonald's crowd was known to place bets on how long it would take Ray, crouching in front of the sideview mirror of his pickup, to find the ideal angle. Yep, no missing that guy in a crowd at a muskie fishing expo.

DESPITE A TWINGE of jealousy, Osborne had to smile. Better even than catching bluegills, the privilege of wearing Ray's hat would have made his grandson's day.

Picking up another slice of pizza, Osborne followed Mallory into the den. "So what's this big idea that's probably gonna cost some poor sucker like me a couple hundred bucks?"

"You tell him, Ray," said Mallory, turning to the fishing-guide grave digger who was always just this side of a million dollars. She looked up at Ray with eyes too happy for her old man. Osborne harbored a nagging worry that his daughter's crush on Ray could turn serious someday.

He had confessed this worry to Lew late one night as they waded into the Elvoy for brook trout. Her response had been no help at all: "Give it up, Doc.

That's none of your business. Mallory's a big girl." And so he tried…but still.

"FawnCam," said Ray, beaming.

Osborne stared at him. "Yeah?" he said, waiting. But Ray just beamed. Mallory beamed.

"What the hell are you two talking about?" said Osborne, glancing from one to the other. He was so tired, he had to be missing something obvious.

"It is too cool, Dad," said Mallory. "Ray has these video cameras from the DNR that he's going to attach to the heads of fawns—so you can see what they see as they move through the woods with their mothers. Incredibly close observation of deer families in their natural habitat. Not like a zoo or one of those wildlife parks, but—"

"The first *ever*…reality nature show," said Ray.

"He's right, Dad. The way it works is Ray sets up his equipment by corn feeders so when the does bring their fawns to the feeders, there's a receiver and VCR right there that can wirelessly download the video. Simple."

"Yep, Doc, I already know the corn feeders I want to use. Mason told me when she was kayaking up Secret Creek that she and her mom saw lots of does with fawns and I know a guy who's got a feeder in there already. I figure four feeders max. That'll give us plenty of footage."

"Better than bird-watching, Dad," said Mallory. "I guarantee. This is a cool idea."

Osborne chewed, then said, "What do you do with the footage you get when they run into cars?" He swallowed his last bite of pizza. "Or do you need a little blood and guts to spice it up?"

"Har-de-har-har, Dad," said Mallory, giving him the dim eye. "We're serious. We'll make DVDs and sell them. Parents, tourists, schools—people will line up for this! I'll handle the marketing, Ray can do the production. First thing, we're going to get a Web site up so people can see excerpts and order the DVDs—"

"Hey, kiddo, slow down," said Osborne.

"And we'll work with Sharon Donovan to sell on eBay, too."

"I thought you were in graduate school."

"Jeez, Louise. Dad, you're no fun. I'll do this on the side, no big deal."

"So whaddya think, Doc?" said Ray, eyes alight with excitement as he straightened up and thrust his hands deep into the pockets of his fishing shorts. "Not…too bad…an…o-p-p-p-or…tun…ity… Right-o?"

"Oooh, I don't know about that," said Osborne, in spite of the risk at hand.

When Ray was in good humor, he had the ability to torture those around him with a delivery so slow it was alleged by people who knew him well that he spoke at the pace of a pregnant snail. And though Osborne was in no mood for a Ray-paced argument, he wasn't willing to concede, particularly in front of Mallory, that this FawnCam thing could work.

"*I* have a question. How the hell do you attach a camera to the head of a fawn? That is a very small animal and one with no antlers…"

"Sheesh—e-e-e-asy," said Ray with a flip of his hand that implied Osborne had just asked the dumbest question he'd ever heard. "We put the camera in a bag…and hang the bag…around the fawn's…neck." As if he were the fawn, Ray pressed the fingers of his right hand against his chest.

Osborne studied the faces of his daughter and his neighbor before saying, "You're serious—a fawn carrying a purse with a camera in it. Doesn't that strike both of you as a bit goofy?"

"Dad, you're crabby. This works. The DNR is already doing it for research. Granted they're working with mature animals, but using the exact same method—and Ray's got a friend at the DNR who will let him borrow a couple of the cameras they aren't using."

Osborne knew he was being testy. Now that he thought about it, he *had* heard something about the DNR project and it could be that Ray *was* onto something. And if he was, then maybe—someday—he *could* support a wife and children.

"Okay, okay," said Osborne, raising both hands and backing off. "I give up. You're right. Plus this old man is too tired to think straight anyway."

"Dad…" Mallory turned a sympathetic eye on him. "You look beat. Why don't you get yourself a good night's sleep and we'll talk more in the morning—'cause it *is* a great idea. And I *am* going to help Ray and I may even invest some of the money I make on eBay in this."

"Oh," said Osborne, his worst fears realized. He decided to keep his mouth shut and just go brush his teeth. Pausing at the doorway, he said, "Mallory— what's an SBF? You and your sister were talking about it this morning…"

"None of your business, Dad," said Mallory without turning away from the computer screen. "Time for bed, remember?"

Osborne shrugged. Okay, he'd ask Erin. She'd tell him. "Ray," he said, ready to close the door to the den behind him, "what time are you planning to be back up on Moccasin Lake?"

"Oh, around six, six-thirty—" Before Ray could finish, the phone rang.

Mallory reached for the cordless. She listened to the caller, then handed the phone to Osborne. "For you, Dad. Someone named Fern Carstenson. She says you left a message at her office that she had to call tonight."

"WE ARE SO *SHOCKED*, Dr. Osborne," said Fern, sounding breathless. "The staff said Nora worked third shift last night and was just as calm and capable as ever. I mean, golly, she was a lovely, lovely person. I just—well, what is it that *we* can do?"

"Answer a few questions if you have a minute, Fern. I'm assisting Chief Ferris with the investigation and during a meeting with Mrs. Loomis's son, Russell, earlier this evening, he said his mother had had a problem with one of your customers, that she was quite upset with the situation—"

"Oh, for heaven's sake, I doubt that was anything. We have little brouhahas with customers all the time. The staff is trained to handle those and it's always the usual complaints—someone's order was stolen from their porch or their box was damaged. That kind of thing."

"That's not what Mrs. Loomis told her son."

"Well, Dr. Osborne, then I imagine she may have overreacted to a customer service issue. Lack of experience, you know. This happens with our new hires."

Osborne resisted the urge to tell her he wasn't interested in what she might "imagine." Instead he said, "Fern, Chief Ferris and I need to hear the tape of the call that bothered her. So you tell me a good time to do that tomorrow—late morning would be best for us."

Silence. Then Fern said, "Dr. Osborne, I don't know that we can locate that tape. Do you have any idea how many hours of taped calls we have here? Universal Medical Supplies takes phone orders from fifty states and four countries. Asking me if we have a tape of one phone call is like asking Wal-Mart if they have a video of every car in their parking lots."

Osborne couldn't believe his good fortune. The moment felt as good as when he'd caught a forty-four-inch muskie on a surface mud puppy when all his buddies were insisting he cast a bucktail. "This may frustrate you, Fern," he said, "but Wal-Mart does exactly that."

"They can't possibly."

"I happen to know they do," said Osborne. "My daughter Erin was shopping at the Wal-Mart in Green Bay two months ago. Someone backed into her car in the parking lot, did fifteen hundred dollars worth of damage and drove off. It took the store a day to run through their security tapes but, believe it or not, they found the sequence showing Erin's car being hit. Got the license plate of the car that did the damage and turned it over to the police."

"You're kidding."

"Mrs. Carstenson," said Osborne, adopting the tone he'd used on patients demanding emergency care even though they had never bothered to pay their bill for dental work done the previous year, "it's after ten and I am in no mood to argue with you. Now, Russell told me that his mother said she met with two supervisors last week to alert them to having overheard a caller being threatened with physical violence. She was concerned that someone's life was at risk."

"*Last week* this happened? Oh, wait a minute," said Fern. "I've been running training workshops since last Wednesday and I may have missed something. Do you mind holding?"

"Not at all."

She was back in less than a minute. "Dr. Osborne, I'm going to put you on the line with our third shift manager—and my most sincere apologies. There *was* a problem last week. I am so sorry but I did not know about it—afraid I'm behind on reading our call center reports. Rick Meyerdierk is here and he's been handling the situation."

Meyerdierk didn't wait to hear Osborne's request. "We have the tape," he said without hesitation. "I've heard it several times and it's had me worried, too. So you think this is somehow connected to whoever killed Mrs. Loomis?"

"It's too early in the investigation to say," said Osborne. "But we're looking at all possibilities and we know this incident had her very worried. Were you able to check on the caller, this person Nora thought might be harmed?"

"No, that's the problem. The person placing the call used a prepaid phone card that the phone company wasn't able to trace—and hung up before the operator came on the line to take their order. Dr. Osborne, we will accommodate this investigation in every way we can. You tell me a time that works for you and Chief Ferris to listen to the tape. You'll want to do it here so you can use our equipment. The detail on that tape is not easy to hear."

AFTER SETTLING ON A TIME that he hoped would work for Lew's schedule, Osborne managed to get his teeth brushed, pajamas on, and Mike bedded down on the floor beside him. Not even the murmur of voices from the den would keep him awake.

Before falling asleep, he let his mind drift back through the day, ending with the happiness and excitement on the faces of his grandchildren. That Mason— so pleased with her kayaking. And what was it she had said about going up Secret Creek and finding treasure? He had to remember to ask her about that. It'd be fun to know Mason's idea of treasure.

With that thought, he let the moan of the wind through the pines put him to sleep.

FIFTEEN

"THE VICTIM FOUND in the water died of manual strangulation—confirmed by significant bruising on both sides of the trachea," said Dan Wright, the only one of the Wausau boys who had shown up for the 7:00 a.m. meeting. The other three, having worked late into the night, slept in. Also, being the youngest, Dan was low man on the totem pole.

But he didn't seem to mind. The investigator, whom Osborne guessed to be in his late twenties given his athletic build, youthful buzz-cut and cheerful enthusiasm, was on a personal mission. He had arrived with a briefcase of documents and a small, clear plastic box of trout flies.

After sitting down to the conference table, opposite Lew and Osborne, Dan had placed the box of trout flies on the table in front of Lew. "My girlfriend gave me these," he said. "But I've just started fly-fishing and I have no idea what most of them are. I recognize the two Woolly Buggers—but the rest? The boss told me you fly fish. I was hoping maybe you could help me figure these out?" His eyes begged.

"Well, let me see," said Lew, sounding flattered. She slid the box toward her and opened the lid. "Very nice. Your friend spent a little money—these were tied by an expert." She held the box open toward Osborne. "Look at these, Doc. Who cares if they catch fish—they're beautiful!"

"Lewellyn, have you ever met a trout fly you didn't like?" said Osborne, admiring the tidy rows of miniature works of art.

"I have. But not these. Now, Dan, since these are all dry flies, they'll float on the surface of the water or you may need to dip them in floatant. You know what I'm talking about?" She gave him a questioning look.

"That much I do know."

"Okay, then here in the first row you have…" As Lew named the trout flies and estimated their hook sizes, Dan took notes. His penmanship was cramped but meticulous. Twice he asked for the correct spelling.

Observing his efforts, Lew said, "Dan, if you work that carefully in the crime lab, I won't doubt a single result you give me. But the wise fly fisherman is not a perfectionist. Standing in a trout stream isn't just about matching a hatch or catching a fish, you know.

"It's about focus, about taking time to see and to listen." She handed him the box. "And it's about survival, too. Getting through those rocks and holes and hidden ledges that lurk below the surface—just waiting to rip your waders." The sparkle in Lew's eyes reminded Osborne of how hungry she always was to get into the water, fly rod in hand, anxious to cast and cast and move through the current until she disappeared from sight.

And while he was never certain of the quality of his own casting or his choice of trout fly, of one thing he was certain: she would return. It surprised him every time how the sight of her shadow against the moonlight filled his heart.

"Sounds like you'd rather be fishing right now," said Dan.

"Oh, you better believe it. Maybe later tonight—nah, more likely tomorrow…"

"Well, I hear what you're saying," said Dan with an easy grin. "But I want to start out right."

"Speaking of which—*we'd* better get started." Lew pointed at his briefcase.

"Oh, yes. Sorry, folks, we do have work to do, don't we?" Dan pulled out a sheaf of papers. "I have the preliminary autopsy reports that the lab faxed in late last night. Do you have copies?" Lew and Osborne nodded. And so they had begun.

"BUT I SEE HERE THAT DeeDee Kurlander had water in her lungs," said Osborne as Dan grew close to the end of his review of the pathologists' findings regarding DeeDee Kurlander and Nora Loomis.

"I noticed that, too," said Lew. "What does that mean exactly? Could it be that she was strangled and lost consciousness but died in the water?"

"I've asked about results like that myself," said Dan. "And what I've been told is that drowning is more complicated to determine than most people think. The pathologist doing the autopsy has two theories—either the corpse was submerged for a period of time during which it's possible for the lungs to passively fill with water, or it entered the channel upright and as air escaped, water entered the lungs. That, plus the fact the victim's body had more muscle than fat is why her body did not float. You'll note the examiner states he's confident that that's postmortem fluid.

"Now, as I mentioned earlier, the Loomis woman," said Dan, "had a profound bruising of the skull, with death caused by intracerebral bleeding. Shards found embedded in her skull match the base of the broken lamp that was found nearby. But both victims had strikingly similar avulsions—severe lacerations with tissue torn away from the underlying bone. We're waiting for the test results but we're pretty sure the avulsions on both victims were inflicted by the same weapon—postmortem."

"That's what we thought just eyeballing those punctures and lacerations," said Osborne. "I was reminded of an animal I saw years ago that had been attacked with one of those old wooden muskie gaffs. The kind with the metal hook on one end. I know that sounds bizarre—"

"Could be, could be," said Dan, nodding. "Or an ice pick. There are holes on both victims consistent with the same sharp object. And we're fortunate that whoever killed DeeDee Kurlander didn't reckon on that boat getting in the way. If her body had not been snagged under the log where the action of the boat kept it secured, it's very likely the current would have carried it down to Moccasin Lake where it may not have been found for days.

"Given that it's summertime and the lake is as warm as it is, just a day or two of eagles nipping and those lacerations would have been nicely camouflaged by natural predators. But the pathologist was able to confirm that they were inflicted postmortem, and by a human."

"So if the Moriarty boy hadn't gotten drunk and let the boat drift up the channel, Chief Ferris might have a missing person on her hands—but no dead body, is that correct?" asked Osborne.

"Right."

"Postmortem, huh? You have to wonder about that kind of mutilation," said Lew. "Is someone deranged? I mean, to mutilate a body after death? That's beyond rage or anger. And why two women who didn't even know each other? What's the connection?"

"You've got one sick cookie out there, Chief." Dan gathered the papers on the table in front of him into a neat stack as he said, "We've got the trace evidence bagged and ready for analysis. We should be working on it as soon as we're back in Wausau. At least I will."

Picking up the box of trout flies, he gave it a light shake before stuffing it into his briefcase. He smiled at Lew and said, "Thanks, Chief—I owe you for helping me look like I know what I'm talking about. It's the father of the girl who gave me these that I need to impress."

"Isn't that always the case?" said Osborne. All three laughed.

Standing up, Dan said, "Folks, I know Chuck's not the easiest guy to work with, but you can be sure *I'll* be on the phone with whatever we find ASAP."

"You have my cell number," said Lew.

"Yep." Dan gave a quick glance over notes from his colleagues before placing them in the briefcase. "Did I mention we got nail scrapings from both victims as well as hair samples at both sites? If any of those match up, it might make your job easier."

"One question before you go," said Osborne. "I was puzzled by the lack of lividity on the body of DeeDee Kurlander. Isn't that unusual?"

"Not if the victim was killed so close to water that the corpse was submerged immediately," said Dan.

"Which underscores my decision to hire Ray to scout the bank along that channel," said Lew, pushing back her chair.

At that moment the door to the conference room blew open and three men in business suits rushed in. Right behind them was Marlene, arms waving, headset askew.

"Chief Ferris, I am so sorry," she said. "These guys would not wait. I told 'em you were in a meeting but they ran back here anyway."

"We have a problem," said one of the men.

"That's obvious," said Lew as she ushered Dan to the door. "Dan, thank you and please thank your colleagues for tackling this as quickly as you have. Be sure to tell Chuck I said 'thank you,' too. We'll talk later." She waved him out, then turned.

"Okay, Bob, what's up?" The three were all familiar faces, all presidents of local banks. Each was as clean-shaven, pink-cheeked and shirt-and-tied as the other, but where bankers do their best to exude confidence, these three were so rattled they were vibrating.

"Chief Ferris," said Bob Carlson, taking on the role of spokesman for the three, "you and I know each other since you bank at First National, but have you met Rick Bonds from Mid-Wisconsin?" Carlson pointed. "And Charlie Madson from the credit union?"

"How do you do, gentlemen," said Lew with a round of handshakes. "And are the three of you familiar with Dr. Osborne, our deputy coroner?"

"Oh, sure," responded the three in unison as they plunked themselves into chairs and leaned forward, elbows on the conference table. Having seen two of the men and the third one's wife as patients over the years, Osborne joined the chorus.

Carlson took the lead. "We're here to report bank fraud involving tens of thousands of dollars, Chief. Each of our banks has been hit in the last two weeks. And it's ongoing! We need your help."

"Sorry, fellas, but—"

"Chief Ferris, please—" Carlson raised a hand "—hear me out, okay? The three of us were having drinks at Business After Five last evening—you know the monthly get-together sponsored by the Loon Lake Economic Development Agency—when we discovered that every one of our banks has lost between *twenty and seventy thousand* dollars. For a town this size, that is one shitload of money, Chief."

"FBI," said Lew. "Bank theft is a federal offense and not within the jurisdiction of the Loon Lake Police Department. I'm sorry."

"We know that and we called the FBI," said Carlson. "They're all tied up with Homeland Security issues along the Canadian border. They said it'll be two *weeks* before they can get someone down here!" Carlson's voice broke. Whether from anger or despair, Osborne couldn't tell.

"Chief Ferris," said the banker from Mid-Wisconsin, "would it make a difference if I were to tell you that two of the accounts that were opened and emptied within the last thirty-six hours were in the names of your murder victims? DeeDee Kurlander and Mrs. Loomis."

Lew stared at him. "I knew DeeDee had opened an account with a large amount of money that was withdrawn on what now appears to be the day after she died but—" Lew turned to Osborne. "Do you know anything about Nora Loomis, Doc?"

"I do. You don't because we haven't had a chance to review my notes from my meeting with her son late last night," said Osborne. "And, yes, he expressed concern over a twenty-thousand-dollar checking account that his mother had opened without telling him. And Rick is correct—the money was withdrawn yesterday afternoon."

"Before or after the call from Sharon Donovan?" said Lew. "Gentlemen," she addressed the bankers, "we don't have an exact time of death yet from the crime lab but we do know when Mrs. Loomis's body was found."

"The withdrawal was made just after noon," said Rick.

"In that case, gentlemen, it does make a difference. But difference or not—the reality is I run a small-town police department. Even though I've added two deputies and have the Wausau Crime Lab assisting with these homicide investigations, we are overwhelmed. I don't have to tell you this is the height of the tourist season— with all the problems that brings. I've got my two full-time officers up to their ears in drunk drivers, shop-lifters, teenagers smoking marijuana in the McDonald's parking lot… And that is aside from domestic violence, a flasher at Kribbetz Pizza and tourists doing fifty miles per hour in a twenty-five-miles-per-hour zone. So unless you gentlemen are willing to do some of the legwork—"

"That's why we're here!" said Carlson. "Whatever we can do to help."

A soft trill filled the room and Charlie Madson from

the credit union reached for his cell phone. He checked the number on the digital readout, then listened.

"Thank you," he said, ending the call. He looked at the faces around the table. "People, we have three more accounts opened and emptied. Another forty-seven thousand buckaroos down the goddamn drain. We're looking for an expert counterfeiter, because these checks are clearing the issuing banks. It's the firms they're drawn on whose internal accounting staff is flagging them when they don't match the bookkeeping records. Thank God for electronic banking, or it would take days for this to surface. Chief Ferris, you are looking at three men who could lose their jobs if we don't find a way to stop this. Our banks are FDIC-liable for every penny missing."

"Charlie, call your office back," said Lew. "Check the names on those accounts. Let's see if any ring a bell."

Madson did as she asked. The names were local residents, one woman and two college students. "One of the kids is in the credit union right now filling out a report for us. What's interesting is all three have accounts with other banks that haven't been touched. Each of these was a new account opened within the last couple weeks."

"At least you've got a live one filling out a report," said Lew. "I was starting to worry that every emptied account might lead to a homicide. Tell me this. Are the accounts opened in person and do we have a description of the party opening those accounts?"

"Well," said Rick, "it's the blessing and the curse of electronic banking. The accounts are opened electronically but the deposits are made at busy drive-ups. As are the withdrawals. As best we can tell, whoever is doing this uses one of the drive-up kiosks that are a distance from the teller windows and they do it during daytime rush periods. The glare off the car windshields makes the security camera worthless. Also, they withdraw the money in increments so that activity isn't flagged until the account is empty. Is that how it's been happening at your banks, fellas?" He looked at the other two bankers, who nodded in agreement.

"But not any longer," said Bob. "We've closed down all but our two closest kiosks and we're taking no significant deposits into new accounts via the drive-ins. Still, it's hard to police everything.

"This time of year with people buying property, changing jobs, kids going off to college—we open so many accounts every day that my staff does their best just to get the paperwork filled out and filed with the deposit. They really don't pay too much attention beyond making sure the check looks legitimate—and these are very sophisticated operators. The checks may be fraudulent, but the way our system works you can't tell that for several days. Plus, they're using the names and Social Security numbers of real people with good credit records."

"Okay, gentlemen," said Lew, "here's what you do. Go back to your offices, contact each of the people whose names are on those emptied accounts and list all personal information you can think of—we're looking for a pattern."

"I have a suggestion," said Osborne. "This reminds me of when dentists in the region would see an outbreak of bacterial infection like 'trench mouth.' We would check to see what restaurants and bars our patients had been patronizing. Any overlap and we knew who wasn't putting soap in the dishwater."

"That's a good point," said Carlson, getting to his feet. "We should find out where these people have been in the last few weeks. Maybe, what—the last month or so?"

"I've got my staff flagging every new account that's been opened recently," said Rick. "I think we should be checking with those folks, too."

"And keep calling the FBI," said Lew in a petulant tone, "because this is really their job."

Minutes later, as Lew and Osborne were hurrying out of the building for Moccasin Lake, Marlene waved Lew aside. "You know you've got that appointment at three today with the firearms rep from Duluth, Chief. Whatshername—Gretel Sandersson."

"Oh, darn," said Lew, stopping at the door, "I forgot all about that. Marlene, please, would you give her a call and reschedule? There is no way I can handle that today."

"Who's that?" asked Osborne as they climbed into the police cruiser.

"Oh, Gretel somebody," said Lew. "In a weak moment I agreed to let her stop by and demonstrate the firearms that other law enforcement agencies are buying. She reps for three different companies. And if there is anything I don't want to do right now, it is waste time looking at guns I don't need."

SIXTEEN

THE PARKING LOT for the Moccasin Lake public landing was packed with SUVs and boat trailers. Not to be missed in one row was a beat-up, blue pickup with a silver-chromed walleye leaping from the hood. "Excitement, Romance and Live Bait: Find It Fishin' with Ray" read the hand-painted bumper sticker peeling from a battered rear bumper. Parked nearby, on a patch of grass along the county road, was a pollen-dusted, forest-green Honda Accord.

"I've seen that car before," said Osborne, turning as Lew pulled past the Accord, "but I can't remember who it belongs to." He was still thinking about the car as they jogged across the lot to the ramp where Ray had moored the police boat after lashing his canoe to one side.

"I want to go up the channel to the bank where the Moriarty pontoon is anchored," said Lew, "and do a walk-through now that Wausau is finished with it. Then, Ray, Doc and I will bring the police boat back here while you work your way up the channel in the canoe. Guess you got a late start, huh?" Lew paused, cocking her head at Ray. "Did you *have* to wear that shirt today?"

Ray glance down, puzzled. It was obvious he hadn't given much thought to what he pulled on that morning,

which was out of character and prompted Osborne to
worry over where and how he had spent the night—not
to mention why he had slept in after saying he would be
here by six-thirty. The T-shirt, navy blue with white let-
tering, laundered and in decent condition, was emblazoned with the legend: "Women Want Me, Fish Fear Me."

"Yikes, sorry about that," said Ray, sounding not in
the least bit sorry. Instead, eyes serious, he jerked his
thumb toward a figure hunkered off to one side of the
parking lot. "You need to know we got company."

Marcy Kurlander, her face pale over a loose black
tunic that she wore with jeans, raised her hand in an
attempt at a wave. Now I know where I saw that car,
thought Osborne.

"Marcy—" Lew's voice had an edge to it "—what are
you doing here?"

"I wanted to see where it happened." Marcy pushed
herself away from the fence she had been leaning
against and walked toward them.

"We don't know yet. All we have is the location
where your daughter—where DeeDee was *found*."

"That's what I want to see."

"Chief Ferris, if the Wausau boys are done up there,
is there any reason she shouldn't be able to?" said Ray.

"Mr. Pradt," said Lew, "when I need your opinion I'll
ask for it."

"I just thought—"

Lew raised a hand and Ray shut up.

As Marcy neared the boat ramp, Lew said, "How are
you doing, Marcy? Were you able to get some sleep?"

"A little. I had a dream about the person who killed
DeeDee."

"Oh…sorry to hear that," said Lew, giving the woman's shoulders a quick, sympathetic squeeze.

"It wasn't a nightmare." Marcy's tone was matter-of-fact. "Have you heard if the autopsy has been completed, Chief Ferris? I talked to the funeral home. I want to be there when they arrive with DeeDee, but they said they didn't expect her to be released until this afternoon."

Lew turned to Osborne, a thoughtful expression on her face. He knew what she was thinking: was this a good time to share what had surprised them in the preliminary autopsy report?

"Tell you what, Marcy. I see no reason for you not to come along. But I want you to remain in the boat while we do the walk-through and agree to return with Dr. Osborne and myself. Ray will be working the channel, trying to track where your daughter's body may have entered the water."

"What does that mean?" said Marcy, stepping into the police boat behind Lew and Osborne as Ray settled into the driver's seat. Lew motioned for Marcy to take the seat beside her.

"It means she was…" Lew struggled to find the right words.

"Dead before she hit the water? No water in the lungs?" Marcy spoke with the crispness of a career nurse.

"That's not entirely true… The cause of death was strangulation before receiving the contusions around the head and the neck. We doubt she was aware of anything after she lost consciousness."

"But she certainly knew who her killer was," said Marcy. "You can't tell me she didn't know that."

The inboard engine at a low hum, Ray eased the boat

toward open water. Lew caught Osborne's eye and gave a slight nod. She was going to tell Marcy the news from the autopsy that had been a surprise to both of them. Osborne held his breath.

"Marcy," said Lew, "were you aware that your daughter was pregnant?"

The look on Marcy's face answered the question. She was stunned.

"The pathologist guessed DeeDee was about twelve weeks along," said Lew. "Any idea who the father might be?"

Marcy shook her head, speechless for a long minute. "No…I don't know. DeeDee didn't say she was seeing anyone seriously. But…um…we were never chummy that way, not like some mothers and daughters. She didn't share details. I knew she was having lots of dates this summer but no one…"

"Oh, God." Marcy dropped her head into her hands, then said in a muffled voice, "You're telling me I lost my daughter *and* her child? Oh…" She curled into her body and turned away, her face toward the water.

No one spoke as the boat arced north toward the channel. As they slowed for the NO WAKE markers, Marcy straightened up as if she had come to a decision. Her chin thrust forward and her eyes were free of tears. "Dr. Osborne," she said, looking over at Osborne and speaking in a level voice, "something I forgot to tell you for the death certificate—DeeDee was baptized Deirdre."

"An easy correction to make," said Osborne. "What a beautiful name."

"Irish, isn't it?" said Ray, slowing to guide the boat into the channel.

"A beautiful name for a beautiful girl," said Marcy, with a ghost of a smile. "Since she was three years old she insisted we call her DeeDee, though." Marcy's eyes settled on Lew. "Chief Ferris, how did you deal with that boy who killed your son?"

"I… Well, you know—no one's ever asked me that question before," said Lew, a stymied expression on her face. After a thoughtful pause, she said, "I guess…for the longest time, I didn't. I couldn't think about the kid without wanting to scream…or do something worse. My rage was… Well, it wasn't healthy and I've never blamed myself for feeling that way. But I didn't want to spend the rest of my life like that.

"Then one day I heard how the kid's life was going— which was not well—and I felt sorry for him. Guess in a way I was able to forgive and…move on. Life since has been okay, Marcy. The sorrow is there, always will be, but I have ways of holding on to my son."

"Like how?" As she asked the question, Marcy's gaze lingered over the water.

"He loved to help me put the garden in every spring. When he was a little tyke, I let him plant the onion shoots. So every year I plant those onions and I think of Jamie. I make it a point to work in my garden one evening a week—that's my time with my son. If that sounds crazy, maybe I am, but my garden—and those crazy onions—have made it possible for me to forgive."

Marcy gave a tight laugh and shook her head. "Forgive? Forgive. Oh, God, right now forgiveness is one cheap grace."

Lew shrugged. "I know."

"Yes…well—" Marcy's shoulders sagged and she

leaned sideways to trail one hand in the water, a thoughtful look on her face "—I appreciate what you just told me. Maybe I can find something like your garden that will work for me." She looked at Lew as she said, "You're probably the only person I know who understands how I feel right now."

Lew nodded, saying nothing.

"Would it be out of line for me to invite you to the funeral Mass and the wake for DeeDee? I'm not sure when it'll be yet."

"Marcy," said Lew, "it would be a privilege."

SEVENTEEN

TWO HOURS LATER, Osborne found himself standing in one room of Bert Moriarty's summer home, a summer home with six river-rock fireplaces, a private five-hundred-acre lake and a seven-vehicle garage, its doors open to display two Mercedes, matching Range Rovers, one Jaguar convertible and a white Toyota pickup. Contemplating Bert's toys—and pictures of his toys—Osborne found himself wondering if Bert put family and career ahead of fishing, hunting, golf and dogs—or vice versa.

The long, narrow space, which Bert had referred to as his "den," opened off a living room so vast it might have housed the Loon Lake Country Club. It was paneled in some exotic wood that Osborne didn't recognize. Anchoring one corner of the room was a massive desk of the same wood, on which rested a flat-screen computer. In the center were two curved leather sofas facing a floor-to-ceiling (or so it seemed) television screen built into the wall. Four captain's chairs (again the strange wood) surrounded a felt-covered poker table, behind which was a window facing west across Bert's very own Lynx lake.

"How many millions do you think they spent on this place?" whispered Lew as they wandered through the room, waiting for the Moriartys to appear. Bert had greeted them at the door, ushered them into the den, announced that Audrey, his wife, would be down shortly and excused himself to complete a phone call. That was twenty minutes ago. And while Lew kept a nervous eye on her watch, Osborne didn't mind the opportunity to look around. And there was plenty to see.

The paneled walls held clusters of framed photos, which included one of Bert on a golf course with men Osborne assumed to be famous (and one golden retriever in a golf cart); Bert in hunting and fishing camps with more men Osborne assumed to be famous (*two* goldens in most of those photos); Bert with his son (just one golden); and Bert with a woman whom Osborne assumed to be Audrey (no dogs). The woman was as tall as Bert but very slender. Her face was a narrow oblong, but a wide smile softened the sharp features.

"If Moriarty doesn't show up in five minutes," said Lew, checking her watch yet again, "I'll have to move our meeting at Universal Medical Supplies back an hour."

Just as she spoke, Bert appeared in the doorway, followed by a woman simply dressed in black slacks and a long-sleeved white blouse. The only jewelry she wore were gold hoop earrings, set off by the dark hair she had pushed back behind her ears. She was, indeed, the woman in the photos, but where that woman radiated happiness, this version carried herself with a haughty aloofness.

After enduring a round of handshakes, she parked herself in a chair at the far end of the room, crossed her legs, crossed her arms over her chest and waited. It struck Osborne that she had positioned herself as far from her husband as possible.

"My lawyer will be here shortly—another five, ten minutes or so," said Bert, taking the chair at his desk and beckoning Lew and Osborne toward the sofas. "I really prefer we not discuss anything relative to the death of that young woman until he arrives."

"Whether or not you choose to reply to anything I say is entirely up to you," said Lew, "but Dr. Osborne and I do not have time to wait for your lawyer." She checked her watch. "We're due somewhere else in less than an hour."

"So what's so important you have to see me right now?" said Bert.

"Earlier today we got the preliminary results of the autopsy on DeeDee Kurlander," said Lew. "Given what we've learned, I have reason to think that you may be able to help us with this investigation. But I think it would be best if we met with you in private on this matter…"

Bert tipped his head toward Audrey. "Sorry, dear, I thought they wanted us both in on this."

"I'm not leaving the room," said Audrey, her head held high like that of an eagle on alert for carrion. "Anything that concerns Bert concerns me—and my lawyer is due any minute as well."

"You *both* have lawyers?" said Lew. "May I ask why?"

Audrey stared at Bert, who said nothing, just kept twirling a pen in his right hand. "That ball's in *his* court," she said. Still Bert said nothing.

"Well, okay, whatever the deal is, you folks can share what I have to say with your legal team," said Lew. "We're here because the autopsy report indicates

DeeDee was three months pregnant at the time of her death—"

"Now just you wait a minute," said Bert, interrupting. "If you have any intention of pinning her pregnancy on my son, I guarantee you I can prove that that young woman was having sex with other people."

"We do know *that*," said Lew, her voice soft and firm.

The room went quiet. Very quiet.

"Bert," said Lew after thirty seconds had passed, "do you want to tell us about it? I take it you were aware of the pregnancy…." She kept her eyes on Bert. Her manner was direct but not threatening. Osborne had seen her do this before, and every time he admired her skill at letting people know that she knew the truth and they had a chance if they did the right thing. Bert didn't have to answer—but he did. He tossed his pen onto the desk, a gesture that was followed by an explosion from the other end of the room.

"No, no, no, no, Bert! I can't believe you did this." Audrey, eyes closed, tone mocking, wagged her head as she said, "I knew you were seeing someone, but that cheap little girl?"

"Audrey," said Bert, "maybe it's time you left the room."

"Are you kidding? I want to hear every word—I don't want to miss a thing you say."

"That's a first," said Bert. He set his lips in a thin line as he said to Lew, "I prefer to say nothing unless my lawyer is present. I'm sorry. If I thought I could help in any way, I would—but…I…" He shook his head.

Audrey stood up. "Chief Ferris, could I have a

word with you—in private, please?" It was a directive, not a request.

"On the condition that Dr. Osborne joins us," said Lew. "I make it a practice to always have two parties involved in any discussions related to a homicide investigation."

"Fine," said Audrey. "Follow me."

She opened a door down the hall from Bert's office. Inside was a large empty room with white walls and wood flooring. The only furniture was a fax machine on a stand in one corner and a floor lamp in the other. "I moved my things out last week," she said with a slow, sly smile. "Do you think he noticed?"

"I take it you and Mr. Moriarty aren't getting along," said Lew.

"Bert will be served with divorce papers shortly," said Audrey with an impatient wave. "All I want to know is how long I have to stay here. I have an interior design business to run in Chicago and the last thing I need is for Bert's situation to impact that."

"At the moment," said Lew, "I prefer that no member of the Moriarty family leave Loon Lake until we've completed our initial investigation. That includes you, your husband and your son—"

"Robbie is not my son."

"Until I've had the opportunity to sit down with each of you, with or without your lawyers, I need you to remain in Loon Lake."

"And how long will that take?"

"Another day or two, maybe longer. I don't know yet."

"All right." Audrey sighed. "I'll move into the guest-house." She rolled her eyes. "I am so tired of that man. I knew something idiotic like this would happen."

"Criminal is a better word," said Lew.

"Whatever."

"Mrs. Moriarty—" said Osborne.

"Spencer. Audrey Spencer—I didn't take Bert's name."

"Ms. Spencer, is there any connection between your divorce and this case that we could discuss without jeopardizing anyone's legal rights?"

Audrey crossed her arms over her chest and stared out a window before saying, "Too much History Channel. That and the fishing catalogs."

"Sorry," said Osborne, "I don't get the connection."

"He bores me out of my mind," said Audrey. "The only books he reads are the fishing catalogs—oh, excuse me, and the gun catalogs. When he's not doing that or golfing, he's glued to that goddamn History Channel."

"Mind if I ask how long you've been married?" asked Lew.

"Five years. And that's four years too long."

"You had a prenup, I assume."

"You better believe I did. That's why my lawyer's here. If our marriage ends due to the involvement of Bert and a third party, I get eighty percent." A crafty look crossed Audrey's face. "I knew what I was getting when I married him."

THEY LEFT BEFORE the lawyers arrived. Audrey saw them out. Looking back at her as he climbed into the police cruiser, Osborne noted that Audrey's sharp features had relaxed into a smirk of self-satisfaction.

"That woman is a piece of work," said Lew as they sped back toward town. "I don't doubt she had divorce in mind the day she married the guy."

"Sure sounds like she'll get a good chunk of the Moriarty money," said Osborne.

"I wouldn't put it past her to find a way to get it all—one hundred percent," said Lew. She glanced over at Osborne. "Think about it. If she is supposed to be Bert's alibi for where he was when DeeDee disappeared…"

"As in watching the History Channel?" said Osborne.

"Right. Betrayal may be more expensive than Bert Moriarty ever imagined."

Osborne was quiet as they drove into Loon Lake. In too many ways, Audrey Spencer and her disdain for her husband had reminded him of his late wife. Thank goodness those years were behind him.

EIGHTEEN

HER FOOT HEAVY ON THE accelerator and lights flashing when necessary, Lew managed to get them to Universal Medical Supplies just half an hour late. Rick Meyerdierk met them in the reception area. Small in frame with a wiry build and close-cut, light brown hair, the call center manager appeared to be in his early thirties. And so well tanned, it was obvious he didn't spend his entire day indoors. Osborne knew he'd seen him somewhere before—likely at a bait shop or on the water.

After introducing himself to Lew, Meyerdierk turned to Osborne. "Dr. Osborne," he said, his voice genial in spite of the tense look in his eyes, "we've met. I coach my daughter's soccer team and your granddaughter, Mason, is one of my players."

"Oh, sure," said Osborne, "I thought you looked familiar."

"At our last practice, I suggested to Mason that she consider soccer as a main sport. The kid's got a knack for it, but she insists she's working to become a world-class kayaker."

"Oh, really?" said Osborne with a chuckle.

"Yep, she keeps trying to persuade the team to go kayaking with her one of these days. At our soccer practice last week, she said she discovered a secret passage she wants to show them—that has a big surprise at the end. My daughter's begging to go. You know kids—they love intrigue. We have a game this weekend but maybe next week the girls can work something out."

"Mason would love it," said Osborne. "She's mentioned this amazing discovery of hers a couple times. I need to follow up and see what the heck she's talking about. She makes it sound like pirate treasure, and I can't imagine what it could be since that creek runs up into a tamarack forest that's all wetland. No buildings back in there."

Rick started down the hall. "If you'll follow me this way, folks," he said. "I reserved the review room for us."

He opened the door to a small office holding a round table and four chairs, its walls lined with cabinets. On the table were three sets of headphones. "Dr. Osborne, if you would take that chair and put on the headphones. Chief Ferris, you do the same here, and this is my set. I ran the tape half a dozen times while I was waiting for you and I think it's better if you listen through the headphones than through the speakers—there's some ambient sound you can hear better this way. But before I run it for you, let me explain some of what you're going to hear.

"When a call comes in, if the people in the call center are busy with other calls, the incoming call is put on hold with a message that states 'all calls may be monitored for quality purposes.' Our monitoring starts at that moment so that anything said while a caller is on hold is picked up by the system. As the manager-in-training that night, Nora was instructed to randomly sample the calls holding in order to see if our people taking orders were using the correct greetings and so forth."

"So that's how she happened to be listening to this call?" said Lew. "She wasn't taking the order, just waiting and listening?"

"Correct."

Rick twisted a dial on a console set into the center of the table. They listened.

AT FIRST ALL THEY HEARD was a grinding noise not unlike a coffee grinder. Then a voice. "I told you she won't be there. I'll take care of things," said a dark, low-timbered voice close to the phone. Osborne couldn't tell if it was a man or a woman.

"What do you mean? She told me she'd be there." The second voice, higher-pitched and wheezy, could barely be heard. The speaker sounded distracted.

"Well, she won't. I fired her."

"What!" The distant voice grew upset. "You what? Give me the phone. I'm going to call her and tell her to forget that baloney."

"You can't."

"What do you mean? Oh—no, you didn't." The voice paused. "Don't tell me you lost it with that girl. Last time you did that you ended up with assault and battery charges. Is that what's going to happen? Are we going to get a call from cops next?"

"I—I just wanted to talk to her, to tell her to keep away from you but she started screaming. You know I can't stand people screaming at me."

"What are you telling me? You hurt her? If you did, you'll get us both in trouble. Tell me, goddammit, did you hurt her?"

The dark voice again. "I told you I couldn't help it."

The voice caught in a sob. "I grabbed her, you know— and she…she… All of a sudden she was down and she wouldn't get up. Sorry, sorry, SORRY!" The voice shouted as if backing away or ducking to avoid a blow.

The wheezy voice grew stronger. "You always do it, don't you? You always think you're running my life… Well, you're not. You're *ruining* things—everything. Every goddamn thing you—" The words were followed by a series of thuds, a grunt and sobbing.

"Hello? Hello?" A third voice now. Female, pitched high with worry. "Hello? Do you need help? This is Nora Loomis with Universal Medical Supply—do you need help?" The line went dead.

Lew looked at Osborne, then at Rick. "Why on earth did she identify herself like that?"

"That's the rule," said Rick. "Anyone in the call center who does not identify themselves in the first greeting is penalized—*on their paycheck*. Trust me," he said with a look that made it clear he did not agree with the policy, "they pound it into 'em."

"All right, please play it again…" After the sixth replay, Lew said, "That deep voice—do you think that's a woman? Doesn't sound like it until you hear the sobbing. The other is definitely a man, though. What do you think, Doc?"

"Not sure myself, but whoever it is has a problem with their front teeth—hear that whistle on their 's' sounds?"

"Yea-a-a-h, you're right," said Rick, after replaying the call again. "Bad dentures, you think?"

"More likely poor orthodontia," said Osborne. "Or cosmetic dentistry. If veneers applied to the central incisors are a little too long or too thick, you'll hear that sibilant 's.' Also, listening on tape like this you're more likely to hear it than if you were speaking directly to the person."

"Tell you what I hear," said Lew. "That grinding sound? Sure sounds like a shredder to me. Marlene bought one for the office and it sounds just like that."

"So we have a whistler and a shredder—" said Osborne.

"And a very good reason for Nora to think someone was at risk," said Lew. "Rick, I understand that when you attempted to trace the call, no luck?"

"Right. We checked with our phone company to see if the records would show the originating number. But when they checked, they found the caller had used a TracFone, which is a prepaid cell phone that is impossible to trace." He shrugged. "I wish we could do more. I had a CD made of the tape so you can replay it on your office computers if you need to."

NINETEEN

As Lew and Osborne walked through the main doors of the department, Marlene rolled her eyes toward the conference room. Dropping her voice, she said, "Ray's entertaining…in his hat." You would have thought she was reporting that the mayor's wife had been seen greeting the mailman in her shortie nightgown.

"Oh-h-h," said Lew with a grimace, "I take it you weren't able to reschedule Gretel?"

"She said her cell phone lost its charge just out of Duluth," said Marlene. "I kept trying but no luck. Ray stopped in here on his way back from Moccasin Lake, took one look at her and you can imagine the rest." The trill of a happy robin floated from the conference room. A six-foot-six happy robin. A happy robin with a beard. Again that look from Marlene. "I love the guy," she said, "but jeez, Louise, y'know."

"Did he find anything?" said Lew, shuffling through the notes that Marlene handed her.

"Oh yes, two teeth and a shoe."

"Yes, indeed. Sounds like he found the site where the Kurlander girl was killed?"

"Let him tell you about it," said Marlene, getting to her feet and picking up her purse as the night operator, her niece Laura, walked in. "It's the only reason I didn't put the kibosh on his taking over with Blond Beauty in there."

"Oh, dear, I don't like *this*," said Lew, handing one of the messages to Osborne, who was waiting patiently behind her. He studied the note. It was a message from the owner of Ralph's Sporting Goods: *Marcy Kurlander purchased a box of ammunition for the handgun that belonged to her late husband. She seemed pretty distraught when she was in the store. They thought you should know.*

"That's no good," said Osborne. "On the other hand, it may be she feels vulnerable."

"We'll see," said Lew. "When she calls about the Mass and wake for DeeDee, I'll talk to her about it."

"Keep going," said Marlene, watching over Lew's shoulder. "You've got another good one in that stack—from your banker friends…"

Lew sorted through until she found it. "You mean this one?"

"Yep, they can't wait to talk to you. Seems they found something. Carlson left his home number and his cell phone in case he's in a meeting."

Lew's face brightened. "Boy, would it be nice to move that off my desk."

"NOW WHEN IT COMES to sniper rifles," Gretel Sandersson was saying as Lew opened the door to the conference room, "you can't beat the police version of the Remington M700…" From behind the table where she had just lifted a shiny new rifle from its case, an attractive young woman with a chin-length cap of lemon-yellow hair glanced up as Lew and Osborne walked in.

The conference table was hidden beneath open gun cases. Revolvers, pistols and rifles had been set out with care—along with holsters, cartridges and magazines. It was apparent Gretel had decided not to let Lew's absence get in the way of her sales demonstration. And from the smiles on their faces, it was obvious the seller and her target were mutually charmed.

To his credit, Ray had removed his hat and was listening intently. Osborne could see why. Gretel was a striking blonde, her face lightly freckled and eyes a sparkling blue that spoke to her Scandinavian heritage. Not unlike Lew, she was of medium height with heft on her bones. That made sense to Osborne. If you're going to be selling sophisticated weapons, you better know how to shoot, and that takes upper-body strength.

"Chief Ferris," said Gretel, walking over to Lew and extending a gloved hand, "I understand I came on a bad day."

"I wish we could have saved you the trip," said Lew, shaking her hand.

"Maybe later this week? Your deputy here has invited me to Friday-night fish fry since I have to travel back this way anyhow. You know I'm determined to talk you out of that Sig Sauer of yours. If you'll just *try* one of the new Glock revolvers with the short trigger reach—I have a lot of women in law enforcement who swear by them."

"That's a tough one," said Lew. "What's this about a sniper rifle? Is Ray making unapproved purchases on my behalf?"

"Heavens, no," said Gretel. The more she laughed and smiled, the worse Osborne felt. How would he tell Mallory?

"Hey, Chief," said Ray, "you never mentioned you had an expert marksman coming in today. I can't get over this—we drive out to the shooting range so she can show me the new rifles they're using and BAM! You ought to see her with an M-16. Man, I swear she could drop a bear five hundred yards away with one shot."

Gretel raised her eyebrows apologetically. "Have to admit I was showing off."

"I appreciate you keeping this joker out of trouble for a few hours, Gretel, and I apologize for not being able to spend any more time with you but we're a bit overwhelmed at the moment with two homicide investigations—"

"Ray told me. I totally understand. I'll call ahead on Friday just in case some time opens up. But I've been hearing about FawnCam, which has made my trip worth it. What a concept! I've ordered one of Ray's DVDs for my little niece." Again the enchanting smile directed at Ray.

"Speaking of which, Ray," said Lew, "Doc told me about this new enterprise of yours and I was wondering if you might have enough cameras that you could set up one or two around my deer garden? Over the last two weeks, I've had an uninvited guest who leaves a very large paw print. And it's not a bear."

"Sure. I'll put a couple out tonight," said Ray. "What are you thinking? A wolf?"

"That or a bobcat or a mountain lion. I think it's a four-legged critter of some kind. Got out of my truck the other night and saw the animal in the clearing near the barn. But it was dusk and the animal was in the shadows. I expected it to run off when I slammed the door but it didn't flinch. That animal watched me all the way into my house. Struck me as too tall to be a bobcat, but I could be wrong. Hope I'm wrong anyway. Bobcats don't worry me."

"Are you serious?" said Gretel. "I didn't know you had mountain lions this far north."

"Not many," said Ray. "They used to be native to the region, but that was a hundred years ago. Then last summer the DNR got reports of a pair sighted along the Prairie River—they follow water. I doubt you have a mountain lion, Chief. But I'll set up so we can see."

"Once the cameras are on, how soon are you able to see the tape?" said Lew, her hand on the doorknob, ready to leave the room. "My grandchildren arrive next week and I'd sure as heck like to know before they get here whether I have a big cat to worry about."

"Right away. It's all wireless and the monitors are at my place. That's the beauty of it. You just fry up a few bluegills, put your feet up and watch movies."

"That easy, huh?" said Lew.

"Nothin' to it. You can watch in real time or, if you want the tape from the previous day or two, just fast-forward to when there's action."

"Then the sooner the better if you can manage it, Ray. Now, Gretel, if you'll excuse us—Ray, Dr. Osborne and I need to sit down and go over what he found today."

"No, we don't," said Ray. "I finished up early this afternoon, processed my photos, wrote up what I found, then put the photos and report on your desk. Marlene sent the negatives, a copy of the report and all the trace evidence down to Wausau, except the teeth—saved those for Doc. Also, figuring you'll want the Wausau boys to take a look, I taped off and posted the site. You asked me to find where DeeDee was killed—you got it." Satisfied that that was as much information as Lew needed, he turned back toward Gretel.

"Ray…" said Lew, "there's more to it than that. Give it to me in detail. Impress Gretel here with your powers of observation."

At that, Ray gave a self-satisfied shrug of his shoulders and leaned eagerly across the conference table. "The long version is this. First, from the canoe I didn't have to go far before I spotted an area where some young oak branches were torn and grasses had been raked and trampled as though something had been dragged toward the channel.

"So I beached the canoe and found footprints—well-defined in the black-and-white photos. Our guilty party wore sneakers. I followed those back in a ways. And I'll be doggoned if there isn't a sandy road down from the public landing that leads to a campsite quite near the channel. Jackpot! Plenty of evidence—blood everywhere, a shoe that's not a sneaker, two teeth and…tire tracks. Shot excellent photos and with no bad weather due in for a few days, Wausau should have a field day."

"No weapon?"

"No weapon. After I taped off the area, I called our favorite game warden. He promised to keep an eye on the campsite and make sure no one gets near it until you're finished in there. So how's that? Enough detail?" Again, he turned to Gretel.

"I guess so," said Lew, thoughtful. "Can't do anything in the dark anyway."

"Ray," said Gretel, checking her watch, "I need to get on the road. Do you mind helping me pack up here?"

"Does he mind helping you pack up," said Lew with a snort as she closed the door behind her. "Doc, you should head home. It's been a long day."

"I thought we might make it to the river this evening."

"Not with the calls I have to return."

"That's too bad." Osborne started down the hall toward the entrance, then paused. "Lew? If you don't mind, I'm interested in what the bankers found out. How about we order in from the Loon Lake Pub—then you call Carlson."

She gave him a grateful smile. "That's a terrific idea. And I really can't complain about Ray—that's great fieldwork he did today."

"I know," said Osborne, "but some things about Ray never change."

"You mean Gretel."

"I mean he's been hanging around Mallory all week and now this. If he's not careful, he's gonna blow his business venture. Y'know," said Osborne with a shake of his head, "Ray likes to call male-female relationships 'the dance of the porcupines.' Wouldn't you think he could take his own advice for once?"

TWENTY

BOB CARLSON PICKED UP on the first ring and Lew put him on speakerphone. "Chief Ferris, thanks for getting back to me. We've had a breakthrough—"

"You have," said Lew, pulling her chair closer to the phone.

"Yep. About four this afternoon, the three of us met and pooled everything we had been able to find out about our customers opening those fraudulent accounts and—we got it! *Every single person had attended one of the Chamber's job fairs within the last few weeks.*"

"Say that again?" said Lew. She shot Osborne a look of disbelief. "Even Nora Loomis?"

"He's right," said Osborne. "Her son mentioned that she was offered the job at Universal Medical after attending her first one ever."

"Yep," said Carlson, repeating himself. "Every one, male and female."

"So what do you think happened?"

"Well, we certainly don't know how exactly—and we're not accusing the Chamber, of course, but we do see a pattern because the accounts were opened within days of the job fairs. However, not one person was aware of the new account in their name until after the money had been withdrawn. Then, if they did know, it was only because they got a notice in the mail or a call from one of us."

"So money was indeed deposited?" said Lew.

"It *appeared* to be. The checks were drawn on legitimate companies—companies with booths at the job fairs—but in fact they were excellent computer-generated counterfeits. The person opening the account would do so electronically with all the paperwork needed to open an account—right down to birth dates and Social Security numbers."

"And no questions were asked? Even when someone was depositing a check for fifteen or twenty thousand dollars?"

"Ah, but that's what they didn't do. The Loomis account, for example, had twenty thousand dollars in it but three checks had been deposited. The first was for eighty-five hundred and the others were in the five to seven thousand range—the person doing the depositing knew to stay under ten thousand dollars—our red flag for anyone trying to launder drug money."

"Bob," said Lew, "I have difficulty understanding why this sudden influx of money wasn't questioned earlier."

"Chief Ferris, do you realize how many people are moving into this region? People with well-paying jobs, hefty retirement accounts, people from the cities who telecommute, professionals who work in health care. The northwoods economy is booming and our banking community serves the region, not just Loon Lake. We have over a hundred thousand people employed within a hundred-mile radius—"

"And the banks are all chasing the same customers, right?" said Osborne.

"You got it," said Carlson. "Someone walks in with a nice check and says half of it is for moving expenses, you don't question—you jump up and down. You celebrate."

"So we have the job fairs as a link," said Lew.

"At least a starting point. So, Chief Ferris, knowing this, do you still want us to call the FBI?"

"You're required to, but I'll follow up right away regardless. This job fair connection may have something to do with whoever killed DeeDee Kurlander—"

"Sorry," said Carlson, "don't mean to interrupt, but I forgot one more thing you might like to know. The accounts were never opened in their home banks. Just like the accounts we mentioned earlier today, it was always a new account in a new bank."

OSBORNE FLIPPED THROUGH his notes from the interview with the Currys—address, home and office phone numbers, his request that Curry drop off the registration forms completed by people attending the job fairs—everything Lew needed for a warrant.

"You think it's the Currys?" he said.

"I don't know, but they would be the ones having access to personal information, wouldn't they? Even DeeDee's, since they had such easy access to the Chamber's offices. Interesting they never found time to drop off the forms you requested."

"I was adamant," said Osborne.

"I know you were. That's what bothers me."

The judge's offices were in the same building as Lew's, but he'd left for the day. A call to his home and a conversation with his daughter got Lew nowhere—the guy was out, no one knew where he was and he'd left word he wouldn't be home until after nine. She arranged to drop the paperwork by his house and pick it up in the morning.

Lew drummed her fingers, her brow knit with impatience. She picked up the phone and called the number Curry had given as his residence. No answer.

"I don't like this, Doc. What if they skip town tonight?"

"There's one more job fair, Lew—tomorrow in Arbor Vitae. I doubt they'll miss that. Plus—don't jump to conclusions. More people than the Currys had access to those forms."

"DeeDee."

"And her friends, if she brought her work home with her."

Again Lew drummed her fingers, thinking. "Someone could have taken advantage of her to get those files. I don't think it would be Bert Moriarty—he doesn't need to scam banks for money."

"Yeah. On the other hand, that whole crowd she hung out with—that's the age group that knows computers inside and out. Maybe…"

"Well, hell," said Lew, "maybe isn't getting us anywhere."

Osborne checked his watch. It wasn't quite six yet. "Let's do this. If we're lucky, we may catch Ryan still at the Chamber. He worked closely with DeeDee—he may know something."

After a few rings, Ryan answered. Lew shared a few details, enough to ask Ryan who beside DeeDee and the Currys would have access to the job fair registrations.

"Why don't you ask Mr. Curry?" said Ryan. "He and his wife are here—they're getting everything ready for tomorrow's job fair—"

Lew jumped to her feet. "Keep them there, Ryan. Lock the door if you have to and pretend you can't find the key, but don't let those two people leave until we get there. Can you do that?"

"Easy," said Ryan. "They're printing a ton of stuff. If it looks like they're finishing up, I'll trip over the cord and pull the plug. Takes the printer ten minutes to boot up."

TWENTY-ONE

OSBORNE SPOTTED RYAN waiting at the entrance to the Chamber offices as they drove into the parking lot. The only other vehicle in sight was a white Toyota pickup. Glare from the sun made it so difficult to see through the windshield that Osborne couldn't identify the person in the passenger seat.

"Lew," he said as they jumped out of the cruiser, "is that Gwen Curry sitting in the truck? Want me to stay out here?"

Lew started toward the truck, then stopped. "It's a dog, Doc. A malamute maybe."

"You're kidding," said Osborne. "How do you fit those two adults in a truck that small with a dog that big?" But Lew was already at the door, which Ryan was holding open for her.

"They're in the back office," he whispered, stepping out of the way. The boy looked worried. "Dr. Osborne, you won't tell them I told you about DeeDee's lawsuit, will you? When I rode my bike in to work this morning, Mrs. Curry followed me the whole way. Felt weird, y'know."

"Not a word, Ryan," said Osborne with a pat on the boy's shoulder. "I'm sure that was just a coincidence. She was on her way here, too. Wasn't she?"

"No. They didn't get here until half an hour ago.

They always do that—come just when we're about to lock up for the day. I think they wait for Mrs. Rasmussen to leave so she doesn't know how much of the Chamber supplies they use. They're always printing tons of stuff on the color copier and that's expensive."

"So, Ryan," said Lew, "thanks for staying. But I'd like you to leave now. Would you mind?"

The look of relief on the boy's face was palpable. He was out the door before they had started down the hallway.

HUGH CURRY HAD TRADED his sport coat and slacks for grimy khaki shorts that sagged under his butt. A Hawaiian shirt, neon blue, dotted with lurid yellow ukeleles, hung loose over his belly. At the moment, he was kneeling in front of a wheeled trunk into which he was jamming sets of manila envelopes. Scattered around on a formica-topped table beside him was a stack of cords, a laptop computer, rolls of duct tape and a box of tools.

He wasn't alone. Seated at a desk at the rear of the room was Gwen Curry, eyes intent on the screen of a laptop.

"Mr. and Mrs. Curry?" Lew spoke from the doorway. Hugh was so startled he jumped. Gwen looked up, her mouth open, and stared. Hugh was the first to recover.

"Sorry, didn't know you were in the building," he said, bracing one hand on the table as he hefted his weight from the floor. Pulling a used hanky from the pocket of his shorts, he wiped at his face then shoved the hanky back into his pocket. Hands on his hips, he exhaled loudly and said, "Boy, am I out of shape. Whew! Gotta do something about that. So, hey, Dr. Osborne—what's up? And you must be Chief Ferris?"

Hugh attempted to shake Lew's hand but she managed to sidestep the gesture by turning around to close the door to the office.

"Don't know if you've met my wife, Gwen. I know the doc has," said Hugh, voice hearty as he pointed to the woman at the desk. Eyes down, Gwen refused to acknowledge the introduction until she had finished saving or deleting whatever it was that she had on her computer screen. Only then did she close the cover on the laptop, shove her chair back and get to her feet—with an audible sigh of irritation.

"What's up?" she said with a growl as she crossed her arms and stared at Lew and Osborne. There was no trace of a smile, only a distinct air of having been pulled away from something much more important than talking to them.

Osborne couldn't help but notice that the sleeves of her fire-engine-red T-shirt were a little too short and too tight—short enough and tight enough to give her upper arms the bulk of a weight lifter. It didn't help that the shirt ended just above the waistline, exposing an alarming expanse of black legging.

Still, he had to admit the woman's face redeemed the odd proportions of her figure. Once again he was struck by the symmetry of her skull (perfectly round), by the flawless skin under the sleek cap of black hair, by the penetrating gaze of her tiny, black eyes—glinting now in the late-day sun that streamed through the office windows.

"Have had some developments in our investigation of DeeDee Kurlander's death that require a few minutes with your husband," said Lew, genial but businesslike.

"What for?" said Gwen. "I thought we answered all

Dr. Osborne's questions yesterday afternoon." Her brusqueness surprised Osborne. Most people found the presence of Chief Lewellyn Ferris—in full uniform with a badge and a gun—to be intimidating. Immediate accommodation was the usual response. Not Gwen Curry— a mosquito couldn't have gotten a cooler welcome.

"Some issues have come up," said Lew.

"Issues?" huffed Gwen. *"Issues* are bothering you people? Couldn't we deal with those tomorrow?" Pointing at the trunk her husband had been stuffing, she said, "We have at least another hour of work to do here—then finish packing so we can leave at the crack of dawn to make setup in Arbor Vitae. We're expecting three hundred people at tomorrow's job fair and—" she shook one of the thick manila envelopes as she spoke "—each one has to get a packet like this—"

"I said a few minutes is all I need."

"Damn! I can't believe this can't wait till tomorrow." Gwen slapped the envelope down on the desk.

"Mr. Curry—" said Lew, ignoring Gwen's display.

"Call me Hugh," said Curry, "and, please, take your time. Gwen and I can finish up later." He turned away from Gwen as if to avoid the sight of her meant avoiding her wrath. "I'm more than happy to cooperate."

"Thank you—I promise not to take too much of your time, Hugh," said Lew. "And, say, would you mind taking that chair behind the desk?" Gwen's eyes sparked. In order for Hugh to sit at the desk, she had to move out of the way.

"And, Mrs. Curry," said Lew, "if you would sit over there, please."

Lew motioned toward a folding chair pushed up

against one wall. She could have said, "Would you shut up and get out of the way," and it would have had the same effect. Gwen's face clouded with anger as she squeezed her way out from behind the desk.

Finding himself in her way, Osborne stepped back— but not before noticing that the black leggings were still dusted with dog hair. He watched as Gwen plunked herself onto the chair. She crossed her legs, right foot pumping with impatience.

"Now, Doc…" said Lew, pulling out two folding chairs that rested against one wall. She placed each in front of the desk so they could sit facing Hugh. "Would you sit here, please." As if anticipating an argument from Gwen, Lew gave her a pleasant look as she said, "Dr. Osborne is Loon Lake's deputy coroner and assisting with the investigation. He'll be taking notes while your husband and I talk."

"Whatever," said Gwen, foot pumping away.

"Now, Hugh," said Lew, settling into her chair with her own notebook resting on one knee, "I'd like a little more information on these job fairs."

"Sure. Ask away," said Curry, leaning forward on his elbows with his hands clasped in front of him. Sweat glistened across his forehead and once again Osborne could see a slight tremor in the hands, even as they were clasped tight. Gwen might be irritated but her husband was wary. Wary and worried.

"A few basics," said Lew with a smile. "How long have you been running Curry Job Fairs? How do you line up attendees? How do you determine which firms will participate? I mean, aren't job fairs pretty common?

Is there a reason why the Chamber contracted with you instead of another firm?"

"Oh, come on," said Gwen, rolling her eyes, "he went over all that yesterday!"

"Not with me he didn't," said Lew, her eyes fixed on Hugh Curry's face, "and Doc's notes are missing a few details."

"Yeah? What kind of details?" said Gwen, hoarse and abrasive.

"I'm talking to your husband," said Lew. The foot pumped faster.

"Maybe I wasn't clear," said Hugh, "but ours are not run-of-the-mill job fairs. We operate off a business model designed to appeal to Gen Xers—people in their late twenties and early thirties, people who are lifestyle conscious. This is the age group employers in this region are anxious to hire, but these people are less motivated by money—they make *lifestyle* choices.

"So what makes our Curry Recruitment Partners unique is software that I have designed to fit that model. We make it possible for potential employers to maximize contemporary behavior patterns—shortening the time frame for both sides of the employment paradigm."

Osborne kept his eyes focused on his notepad. Listening to Curry spout jargon was almost as painful as sitting through the twenty-first repeat of one of Ray's jokes.

"Fascinating," said Lew.

"A visionary approach," said Curry, unclasping his hands and settling back in his chair.

"No wonder you have such extraordinary turnouts. If I understand what you're saying, Hugh, your firm is a leader in redefining recruitment practices—"

"Boy, are we ever," said Curry, enthusiasm mounting in his voice. "We've introduced a totally new dynamic to the field and it's my software that makes it possible for your Chamber and their members to design a database that will be operational for two years. That database is posted online and it contains all the information needed by people seeking employment as well as profiles of the firms looking to hire."

He dropped his voice. "In fact, it allows potential employers to do full background checks and you don't get that from *anyone* except us."

"Well, I am very impressed," said Lew. "I imagine it takes a great deal of time."

"Not really," said Curry, basking in her compliment. "The applications scan in a matter of minutes. Once the data is entered, the software does the rest. However—" now his tone turned ever so slightly pompous "—our software is proprietary and much too expensive for a small organization like the Loon Lake Chamber of Commerce to purchase, so the Curry Job Fair is the single most cost-effective way to achieve personal interfacing as well as access to a sophisticated database."

"Which comes with a two-year lease," said Lew.

"Right."

"Wow," said Lew. "Now I fully understand why the Chamber is so happy to have you. I imagine you'll be back next year? I hear talks are under way."

"No," said Curry, his eyes suddenly fearful. He darted a swift glance at Gwen, then said, "Don't know where you would have heard that. We're planning to be in North Dakota next spring."

"My error," said Osborne, playing the game. "I thought I'd heard that you offered DeeDee Kurlander a full-time job to continue working in the region. Must have got that wrong."

"You certainly did," said Curry, wheezing. Again, the nervous glance at his wife, who stared straight at him, stone-faced.

"Our mistake, sorry," said Lew. "Maybe what Dr. Osborne heard was that the Chamber would love to have you back when you have time in your schedule." At the sound of her words, Curry appeared visibly relieved.

HER TONE WAS ADMIRING, her technique impeccable. It was a technique that Osborne had observed before. In the flow of Lew's attentiveness, her prey could almost always be counted on to give up information they had not planned to share. Those were the moments Osborne enjoyed the most, just as he loved watching Lew in the trout stream, mending a dry fly across riffles—teasing the canniest brown trout…closer…closer.

SHE CONTINUED TO ASK questions—each generating an answer that underscored Hugh's role as a master of the universe. Beaming, preening and devoted to answering each query in detail, his hands had stopped shaking and the perspiration had vanished. By Osborne's reckoning, the man was now as puffed as a ruffed grouse drumming for females.

"Dr. Osborne mentioned that he asked you for copies of the applications that people had filled out…"

"Sure," said Curry, reaching into the envelope on the desk, "here's a blank one—it shows you all the data we're able to gather and input." He handed the sheet to Lew, who took time to study it.

"This is quite a bit of personal information," she said. "Social Security numbers, bank references—you even have them giving marital status and other personal details that the Feds don't allow the rest of us to ask for when we're hiring."

"Uh-huh. And they all fill it out," said Curry with a smirk. "That's what makes it possible to run those background checks that I mentioned. See, if you look closely at birth dates and such, sometimes you can even figure out their passwords. People tend to be lazy, and that works for us."

"Well, I'm surprised people tell you all this," said Lew. "I wouldn't."

"You don't need a job," grunted Gwen from behind them.

"Now those completed forms," said Lew, ignoring the comment, "I need those, Hugh. I'm interested in tracking all the people attending these last two weeks of job fairs—anyone and everyone who interacted with DeeDee."

"Too late—they've been shredded," said Gwen. "We promise confidentiality. But had I known you wanted them—"

"I specifically asked for those yesterday afternoon," said Osborne, twisting in his chair to confront her.

"You did? I don't recall that," said Gwen.

"Now, wait, hold on," said Hugh. "It shouldn't be an issue—Gwen's input all the data. You can work from our database and get everything you need. Here—" he opened the laptop that was on the desk "—I'll pull it up for you right now."

"Actually, hon," said Gwen, "it's still on the office computer back at the house, I haven't uploaded to the server yet."

"Okay, we'll deal with that later," said Lew. "But now I'm curious—who has access to the database once it's on the server?"

"We do, of course, and the Chamber."

"You mean people here at the Chamber can see all this *confidential* information? That doesn't sound too confidential to me."

Hugh glanced quickly at his wife. "Well, not all—"

"Oh, yes," said Gwen, "our contract calls for that. We assume they will be responsible in how they handle it."

"I see," said Lew. "One last question… How do you plan to handle the lawsuit?"

Astonishment crossed Hugh's face. "Lawsuit?" From the corner of his eye, Osborne saw Gwen's foot pause midair and remain still.

"Yes, we've learned that DeeDee Kurlander was planning to file—or may have already filed—a lawsuit against you alleging sexual harassment."

"I-I-I haven't heard a word about any lawsuit."

"Really?" said Lew. "Perhaps I was misinformed."

"Perhaps you were," said Gwen. "Given the circumstances, there is nothing to discuss—no plaintiff, no lawsuit." She paused, then said, "And for the record— if there was such a lawsuit, it would have been that little shit's effort to blackmail my husband. I'm curious—did you ever meet that girl?"

"No," said Lew, "I did not. But I know she was working hard on the job fairs and felt—"

"She was working hard to meet a man with money, is what she was working on. You couldn't miss it. That girl was so hot she smoldered. When Hugh offered her a bonus, she turned it down—she wanted more, you see. So any lawsuit was just…just…*revenge.*"

"Gwen—"

"Shut up, Hugh. These people need to know about little Miss Perfect. See—" Gwen shook a finger at Lew "—Hugh was blinded by that dumb little blonde but I could see exactly what she was up to. She was all over him like a cheap suit—just like you…"

"Gwennie—" Hugh's voice hit a higher register.

"Just like me *what?*" said Lew.

"Don't you start telling me what to think, Hugh—I know what I saw. And that girl, she's the one who got into the database. She's the one pulled the shenanigans with the banks. Thought she could take the money and run."

"What shenanigans?" said Lew. "I didn't mention anything about banks—did you, Doc?"

Osborne shook his head.

"What do you know about the situation with the banks, Gwen?"

"Just what Hugh told me. He took the call. Hugh, you tell 'em what they said. And all because of one stupid girl."

"I see," said Lew. She paused to look down over her notes, then looked up at both Currys. "Of course, you both knew DeeDee was three months pregnant…"

Osborne didn't even have to move his chair to get a clear view of Gwen Curry's chipmunk eyes—they were fixed on her husband and tight with rage. He doubted Hugh noticed, however. The color had drained from the man's face and for a fleeting moment, Osborne thought he might pass out. The hand that had shown a slight tremor before, now began to shake. Both hands were shaking.

"DeeDee pregnant?" he stammered. He shook his head in disbelief. Then he took a deep breath and sat still, his eyes staring off into the distance. Lew asked a few more perfunctory questions but she had to repeat each one, as Hugh was barely listening.

"YOU BELIEVE HUGH really got a call from the banks?" whispered Osborne as they walked out of the Chamber.

"Not sure. I thought Bob and I agreed they would keep things under wraps until we had all the information. But someone could have not gotten the message. Fact is, they know the banks have been alerted, which is why we have to move on this ASAP."

"You changed the subject from the banks to DeeDee pretty fast."

"And did that ever shake somebody up. Did you see the expression on Hugh Curry's face? He was stricken. And obviously had no clue that DeeDee was considering a lawsuit."

"Caught Mrs. Curry off guard with that bit of news, Lew."

"I just hope Gwen doesn't think we know more than we do," said Lew, keeping her voice low as they approached the cruiser. "This is frustrating, Doc. I can prove they had access to the personal data used to open the accounts but we have no proof they had anything to do with the counterfeit checks used to make the fake deposits. That's why I need that warrant. Even if we don't find checks, I'll bet we find some evidence of counterfeiting—whether it's the paper they use, the software, something. I feel sure of that."

Opening the door and sliding under the steering wheel as Osborne got in from the other side, Lew said, "Think those two are capable of skipping town?"

Osborne gave that some thought. "Maybe… She slipped on letting you know they knew about the banks. I wouldn't be surprised if they were on the road by midnight tonight. Poor DeeDee. Do you think she uncovered the bank scheme and that's why—"

"Could be—which is why we need to track down Judge Richardson. If I don't have that warrant within the hour… We have to find him. And I don't care if that means calling all the restaurants, bars and casinos in the county."

"He could be out fishing."

"Not Richardson—he's the indoor type."

As they pulled into the parking lot, Osborne said, "Did you notice how often Curry would tune his wife out?"

"Can't blame him—it's her way or the highway. She doesn't listen."

"But she runs the show."

"Yep. That she does. She sure does."

TWENTY-TWO

As Osborne and Lew hurried up the stairs toward the
entrance to the police department, Carrie Koronski burst
through the doors and tripped down the stairs to stop in
front of Lew. "Chief Ferris!" she said, out of breath and
talking fast as she pushed her long, blond hair out of her
eyes. "I've been waiting for you and I know you're
really busy—but do you have a few minutes?"

"Something wrong?" said Lew. The young woman's
eyes were clouded with anxiety.

"I don't know," said Carrie. "Maybe. In the middle
of the night last night I remembered something DeeDee
said when she was really, really drunk a couple Saturdays ago. I didn't think much about it then—but it kinda
makes sense now."

"Come on back to my office," said Lew, pointing
down the hall. "We're busy, but not too busy to hear this.
Oh—" Lew stopped and turned to look at Carrie
"—were you aware that DeeDee was pregnant?"

"Kind of," Carrie whispered.

"What do you mean 'kind of'?" said Lew. "You can't
be 'kind of' pregnant."

"She wasn't sure when she told me."

"And when was that?"

"The night I want to tell you about." They had

reached the door to Lew's office. She beckoned for Carrie and Osborne to enter ahead of her. "So you know, huh? Does her mom know?" Carrie's face crumpled, her eyes glistening with tears. "Am I in trouble 'cause I didn't tell you? I just couldn't with her mom there. I couldn't—if it wasn't for sure y'know? Juliana was already so mad at me."

"It's okay. You're telling us now and that's what's important," said Lew, throwing her notebook on her desk and pulling her chair back. She collapsed into it with a sigh of relief.

"Here, you take this chair, Carrie," said Osborne, pointing to one of the two armchairs facing Lew's desk. He glanced over at Lew to make sure she wanted him to sit in, and she gave a quick nod.

Carrie waited for Osborne to sit, too, then said, "I woke up in the middle of the night last night and remembered something that happened two Saturdays ago. Juliana and DeeDee were out that night but I stayed home." She gave a weak smile. "Broke up with a guy I'd been seeing and didn't feel like being around people.

"I was already in bed asleep when I heard DeeDee come in. She was banging around so much I got up to be sure she didn't, you know, light a cigarette and leave it burning or something."

"All that working out and she smoked?" said Osborne.

"Only when she was drinking. I told you about the beer pong contests? Sometimes she got so drunk that when she got home me and Juliana had to keep an eye on her."

"That bad?" said Lew.

"Oh yeah—so drunk she couldn't remember the next day how she got home."

"So this was two weeks ago on a Saturday night?" said Osborne, jotting a note.

"Right. I wanted to get her into bed before anything bad happened but she wanted to talk. Insisted. I could tell she was furious about something and I couldn't keep her from getting another beer either."

"So you were trying to be the big sister," said Lew, sympathizing.

"Yeah, sort of…" Carrie hesitated, then sighed and said, "DeeDee was complicated. She could be hard to deal with when she was drinking. Sober she was great. She could be cute and funny and really, really fun. But drunk she was like this whole other person."

"How so exactly?" asked Lew. "And be specific, Carrie. When I asked you if DeeDee put herself at risk in any way, this is what I meant. Did she do things that could cause someone to want to hurt her? Was she belligerent when she was drinking?"

"More mean," said Carrie. "Mean *about* people, mean *to* people. So mean that if you got in her way when she was drinking, she'd come after you. *Scary* mean is what I'm trying to say. But in the morning, when you asked her if she meant what she'd said—whether it was about you or someone else—she wouldn't remember a thing. So she certainly never apologized. I just hated her when she talked drunk. In fact, Juliana and I had been thinking of asking her to move out if she kept it up.

"See, my dad drinks a lot and he'll act like that. I hate it. I just hate it." The young woman's eyes glistened as she spoke. Her hair was long and loose and every few minutes she would use both hands to shove it behind her ears. "I was starting to hate DeeDee and…and now I feel so bad about that." Osborne tensed. The anguish twisting Carrie's face was familiar. He'd seen that same look on his daughters' faces and he'd hoped never to see it again.

"So that night she came home drunk…" Lew urged her on.

"Right away I could tell she was in one of those mean moods so I sat on the sofa like she asked me to and listened. To humor her, y'know. That's when she told me Mr. Moriarty—Bert is what she called him— said he didn't want to see her anymore, but she was 'sure as hell gonna change his life with a big surprise.'" Carrie mimicked DeeDee's tone.

"That's when she told me she thought she might be pregnant. She didn't know for sure, but she'd missed her period two months in a row." Carried paused.

"See, the thing about DeeDee…" Carrie tilted her head up and gazed at the ceiling as if making up her mind. "The thing I didn't like about DeeDee was how she was about money. It was the most important thing to her. Whenever she got blasted like she was that night, she would always go on about how you have to marry money or you end up like her mom. Then she would swear that she would never end up like her mom—all alone, living paycheck to paycheck. She was a broken record about it."

Carrie's eyes searched Doc and Lew's faces for approval. "You can see why I couldn't let her mom hear something like that."

"So she wasn't seeing Bert anymore? Did he know about the pregnancy at that time?"

"Yes. DeeDee had decided to tell him she was pregnant even though she wasn't sure. She wanted his reaction and it really surprised her when he told her he would pay for an abortion, but he had no intention of asking his wife for a divorce, much less marrying DeeDee. Oh God, you had to see her face that night to know how furious she was. It's when she decided to do what she did with Mr. Curry. She thought she could make Bert jealous. And if that didn't work, she was going to convince Mr. Curry it was his baby and get him to marry her. He was infatuated with her and she knew it."

"Really," said Lew. "So you're saying she was deliberately leading Hugh Curry on?"

"Talking drunk that's what she said—and, man, she had it all planned out," said Carrie. "To me, anyway, it seemed like the minute she thought Bert was dumping her, she just got more determined to get married. She had this evil little smile when she said it, too. 'I don't care who the hell it is as long as he's rich. I'll get married, have the baby, then get a divorce and leave with all the money.'"

"I don't think it's quite that easy," said Lew.

"You couldn't tell DeeDee that," said Carrie. "She was convinced she could pull it off."

"But one of the people she was working with at the Chamber told us she was planning to file a sexual harassment lawsuit against Curry," said Osborne.

"Oh, she talked about that, too," said Carrie. "She was going to use that for leverage, so if Curry didn't do what she asked, she could hold that over him. She thought it was so clever that she had him wrapped around her finger—other people could see he was doing things that would appear inappropriate. What they didn't see was her encouraging it."

"But that man is so…so…so unattractive," said Lew. "I find it hard to believe—"

"Money. The guy's got 'tons' according to DeeDee." Carrie gave a grandiose wave of her hand as she mimicked her roommate. "According to DeeDee, she had him on his knees. 'Do I have him roped or what?' she'd said. 'Right by the old schnoz.'

"But like you just said, Chief Ferris, I remember saying to her—Yea-a-h, but you still have to sleep with the guy."

"What did she say to that?" said Lew.

"One word. 'So?' But, see, the money made it okay. Don't ask me how she knew, but she was convinced he was worth at least a million, most likely more. She told me that in one day she had watched him withdraw nearly a hundred thousand dollars from different accounts."

"Do you think it occurred to her he might be doing something illegal?"

"No-o-o. She thought maybe he gambled."

"Did Curry ever come to your house?"

"A couple times, but she would always step outside and see him. Except one night he scared the living daylights out of us. Our neighbor called to say there was a man standing outside DeeDee's window. That was creepy and it scared her, too. Later she laughed it off. Most times they'd talk in his truck. At first Juliana and I assumed it was all business—but here's what I remembered in the middle of the night last night. First it was the drunk talk about tricking Curry into marrying her. And then I remembered something else.

"It was the night before she…the night of the day before Robbie's party. She got several calls from Mr. Curry that evening. I didn't think too much about it at the time because there was always a flurry of phone calls from him right around one of the job fairs. The guy was fanatic about checking on stuff both before and after the event—it was always crazy. Whatever bad things I say about DeeDee, she was great at all those details and the arrangements. She really ran those job fairs.

"But I overheard one conversation. The more I try to think back, the more I remember how it made me sick to my stomach to hear her being so…so…seductive on the phone, too. Not professional. Wa-a-y too personal, y'know."

"You're thinking he might have been the person she met at the landing that night?" said Lew.

"Yes, I am." Carrie nodded.

Lew jotted a few notes then stood up behind her desk. "Thank you, Carrie. I'm going to look into this right now." In response to the look on the girl's face, she said, "No, it's okay. You did nothing wrong. Giving yourself time to think things over is not the same as withholding evidence. Just call me on that cell phone number I gave you if anything else comes to mind."

TWENTY-THREE

SHOTGUNS AND BATHTUBS are never a good combination. That, Osborne had learned years earlier when Henry Bloomquist, the elderly dentist whose practice he had purchased, committed suicide in the family home the night before his daughter's wedding. Colleagues pointed to mercury poisoning as a possible source of his depression, but Osborne knew better.

After discussing the patients whose care he was handing over to Osborne, the old man had invited him to the tavern across the street from the dental office. Three whiskeys into their chat, Henry was ready to unload. "I got a miserable family life, Paul," he'd said, slamming his drink on the counter. "And I sure as hell hope it never happens to you. Got a wife and daughter who love the money and despise the old man who makes it. You oughta hear 'em—'you don't dress right, you drink too much, blah, blah, blah.' Hell, they say they're too embarrassed to go to fish fry with me.

"But ya know what?" he said, slurring slightly as he ordered a fourth whiskey. "I'll fix 'em. Just you wait. First, I'm takin' a trip all 'round the world—just me, see. All by myself. Spend a lotta money on the way. Then when I get back…big surprise."

He didn't say what the surprise was. Osborne assumed he was thinking divorce and, in a way, he was. So Dr. Bloomquist did exactly what he said he would. After selling the practice, he traveled for six months. But it was his final trip—the one he took after the rehearsal dinner—that ruined the day for the women in his life. Killing himself in the bathroom of the newly redecorated master bedroom suite that was so important to the mother of the bride made for an awkward wedding day. He could not have better revenged himself.

BUT GWEN CURRY did not appear to have had revenge visited on her. Yes, her face was drained of color and her eyes were red and puffy from tears. And, yes, she seemed stunned. But she was surprisingly calm. The denial and anger, not to mention anguish, that Osborne had come to expect when arriving to perform the duties of deputy coroner on the occasion of an unexpected and sudden death, were absent.

Lew and Osborne had arrived to find her sitting on the stairs of the house they had rented on Mirror Lake, still in her red shirt and black leggings. Saying nothing as they walked toward her, she held out a sheet of paper.

"I had no idea," was all Gwen said, arms crossed and body still, as Lew scanned the page. "I knew he kept copying checks but I thought they were payments from the exhibitors. I had no idea they were counterfeit.

"And that girl…" Gwen dropped her face into her hands, then raised her head with a fierce shake. "Why didn't I pay attention? I should have known, but I trusted… I thought it was all DeeDee, but no, no, no, NO. They were in it together. I'm a fool, such a fool. And now I'm to be blamed, aren't I?"

"Hard to say, Gwen," said Lew, turning to Osborne. "Doc, just to be on the safe side, would you hand me a pair of those nitrile gloves and put on a pair yourself before I hand you this?"

"Sure," said Osborne, "and an evidence bag, too?"

"Yes, thank you. We'll want to keep the chain of evidence tight on this as we enter."

"It's a suicide, not a crime," said Gwen, taken aback.

"Yes, but your husband is confessing to a crime—this piece of paper will be evidence needed by the court and it's my job to see it handled by as few people as possible."

Gloves on and holding the typewritten document at the edges, Osborne read down the page as Lew said, "Gwen, do you know where the money is?"

Gwen raised her hands and dropped them. "No idea. I found Hugh with that—" she pointed to the sheet of paper "—on the bathroom counter. Obviously he did it on the computer and printed it out before… Not sure what to do, I called 9-1-1 and walked out here. Been sitting here waiting is all. Didn't even cross my mind to look for the money. Does that surprise you?"

"No," said Lew. "When someone takes their own life, nothing surprises me. I know it's a shock and I can only try to understand how you must feel."

Osborne glanced up as she spoke. Hugh was a good typist and his message was clear: opening accounts in job seekers' names, depositing counterfeit checks from companies participating in the job fairs, then leaving town before companies and banks got wise to his scheme, he had managed to siphon nearly eight hundred thousand dollars from a dozen banks—four in Iowa, five in Minnesota and three in Illinois where they worked their scam before arriving in northern Wisconsin. And after he met DeeDee Kurlander, it appeared that he had decided it was all for a new life with that young and beautiful woman. *"I loved her, Gwennie. She was so, so sweet and so pretty. And she listened to me. She loved me, too. She said I made her laugh."*

But DeeDee betrayed him. On a night when he had told Gwen he was working late at the Chamber, he had waited for DeeDee to leave the office and followed her, hoping to tell her he had all the money ready so they could run off together—only to see her meet and embrace another man. It was obvious they were lovers.

"All she wanted from me was the money," he wrote. *"She destroyed me. I waited until her lover drove off and then I couldn't help myself. She ruined me!!!! Now the banks are closing in, too. Gwennie, I did love you. I did, maybe I still do. I'm so confused. All I know for sure is I deserve to die. I think that if you show that woman police officer the checks I used she'll know you had no part of this. You'll find them in the cab of my truck, under the backseat. Please, Gwennie, forgive me. You deserve better."* That was it. No signature.

"Want me to check the truck?" said Osborne.

"Later. Let's take a look at the body before the EMTs get here."

"I have to keep this, Gwen," said Lew, as Osborne slipped the confession into the evidence bag she held open.

"I know," said Gwen. She clenched her eyes shut. "Oh God—how he must have hated me. You know—" she raised one hand "—I sensed something was wrong these last few weeks, but Hugh has always been a tense person when the fairs are going on. It's so much work."

"Where will we find him, Gwen?" said Lew. "Dr. Osborne has to confirm the—"

"Master bath," said Gwen, averting her face. "We rent this place so I'm sure the landlord won't appreciate what's happened."

With effort, she pushed herself to her feet. Osborne felt bad but he had a definite reluctance to reach out and help her. "You go ahead. I'll wait in the kitchen. I can't— I can't look at him again."

"You have a dog," said Lew, "in the house?"

"Don't worry about Choppy, he's out back."

"That Ford," said Lew, pointing to a dark green truck parked next to the white Toyota pickup in the driveway. "That is your husband's, correct?"

Gwen nodded and opened the door to the house for them to enter. The wail of an ambulance could be heard in the distance.

TWENTY-FOUR

THE CURRYS' HOUSE was the type of expensive seasonal rental that came fully furnished, including a dock and small boathouse on Mirror Lake. The lake, which branched off the Loon Lake chain, could be reached by canoe or kayak through the shallow stream that Mason called her "secret passage." Too small for the bass boats with their 250-horsepower outboard motors and surrounded with acres of wetlands that discouraged development, Mirror Lake was a popular destination for kayakers and canoeists eager for herons and turtles.

The Currys appeared to be canoe enthusiasts. As Lew had pulled into the drive that ran alongside their house, Osborne had spotted a long metal canoe beached near the dock. A life jacket and a paddle lay on the ground nearby, as if someone, jumping from the canoe in a hurry, had thrown them there.

MOVING PAST GWEN to enter the house, they stepped into a spacious "lodge" room with floor-to-ceiling windows facing the lake. On the immediate left was an open kitchen with a cooking island fronted with a breakfast bar and four chairs. Straight ahead was a large living room with a beamed ceiling and river-rock fireplace. Sofas, chairs and tables were scattered around the room, though they would not be easy to use as they were fully occupied.

The house was crammed with stuff. Every counter, every end table, even the coffee table held piles of paper that appeared to have been set down and shoved around at random. Unopened envelopes, bank statements, bills, brochures, magazines, newspapers, half-eaten cookies, used glasses, used paper plates, crushed napkins, clumps of used plastic wrap, lipstick-smeared coffee mugs and opened beer cans littered the place.

The kitchen sink was crowded with dirty dishes and the counters held even more papers, along with half-empty bottles of gin and vodka. But it was the piles of papers sliding every which way that amazed Osborne. He resisted the urge to walk through the room and straighten up the stacks. As far as he could see, there was only one item in the room currently free of clutter, though he was sure that would change. Just inside the front door and off to the right was a large, unopened cardboard box stamped "Fragile."

Gwen, who had followed them in, walked over to the breakfast bar where she paused to move a pile of stuff onto the floor and hoist herself onto a chair, her back to them. Catching Osborne's eyes, Lew raised one brow in silent comment: *Do you believe this mess?*

"Down there," said Gwen, with a wave toward a hallway that Osborne assumed led to the master bedroom. On their way down the hall, they passed two other rooms also in disarray, with papers strewn about and clothes tossed over chairs.

One appeared to be the office Gwen had referred to, since a long table against one wall held a computer and a cordless phone on its base—along with a slew of discarded bottles, cans, mugs and an open box of chocolate-chip cookies. Shoved to the side of a table holding a printer was a commercial-size shredder that, judging from the contents spilling from a black garbage bag next to it, got plenty of use. But this room did have some order to it. A path through boxes and litter led to an office chair stationed in front of the computer.

Pausing in the doorway to the office, Osborne shook his head in wonder. Any attempt to make sense of the mess in this house would be as challenging as tracking a wounded deer through a cedar swamp dense with dead trees, fallen limbs and treacherous hillocks. He shuddered at the thought of the bacteria growing in the discarded bottles and cans.

At the end of the hall, they arrived at the master bedroom—or at least an unmade king-size bed indicated that was its likely use. An L-shaped nook—intended to serve as a dressing room, though it appeared to be just one more dumping ground—led to a door, which was closed.

"This has to be it," said Lew, smoothing the nitrile gloves tight along her fingers.

Osborne braced himself. The 9-1-1 call had come in just as—in hopes that the search warrant might arrive any minute—he and Lew had finished wolfing down take-out cheeseburgers from the Loon Lake Pub. Right now that seemed like bad timing.

THE SCENE IN THE BATHROOM was unsettling. While the shotgun pellets may not have exited, the blood had. The bathtub and the white ceramic tiles surrounding the tub held a collage of neon-blue fabric, clots of tissue, fragments of hair and teeth, and a human frame recognizable from the shoulders down—all soaked crimson. What remained of the man they had last seen in grimy shorts and a Hawaiian shirt was slumped sideways over the barrel of a twelve-gauge shotgun—a gun that would need a professional cleaning if it were ever to be used again.

After several moments of silence, as he and Lew took in the scene before them, Osborne knelt to do his job. But a careful prodding of the soggy shorts yielded only a small comb and loose change.

"No wallet?" said Lew.

"Nope."

Before leaving the bathroom, Lew used her cell phone to call the Wausau Crime Lab. The EMTs were just entering the bedroom as she was patched through to the pathologist on call. "Yes, we'll need an autopsy," she said, then listened. "Good, I'll have you talk to one of the EMTs so they handle everything correctly, and we'll send the body down first thing in the morning."

Turning toward the three men who had just walked into the room, she said, "Who's in charge here?" After arranging for the lead EMT to call Wausau on his phone for instructions, she made one more call—to Dan Wright on his personal cell phone.

"Dan," she said, "Chief Ferris here. You impress your girl's dad with those trout flies?" As she listened, a smile crossed her face. Osborne found himself grinning at her pleased expression. "Great. Well, Dan, you owe me—right?"

Talking fast in a low tone, she described the events

of the last few hours and Hugh Curry's confession. "That said, Dan, is there any chance you could make it up here tomorrow? I sure could use the help…great. Good. See you at ten in my office."

GWEN HAD CLEARED HERSELF a more comfortable spot on one sofa, where she now sat, quiet and composed. After moving a few piles themselves, Osborne and Lew were able to find room to sit, too. Osborne started in with the same questions he had asked Marcy Kurlander. Gwen's voice, so abrasive earlier in the day, was now a low purr of grief as she responded. "No need to rush on the funeral arrangements," he said, finishing up. "We don't know how soon they can complete the autopsy."

"What do you mean, autopsy? I didn't ask for any autopsy. It's obvious my husband committed suicide." The purr was gone. Back was the bark—with a hiss. She spoke with a sibilant "s" that Osborne hadn't noticed before. Another case of bad dentistry? He wasn't sure she didn't deserve it.

"State law requires an autopsy when a death is not the result of natural causes," said Lew.

"Oh," said Gwen, "as if everything isn't bad enough already." With a heavy sigh, she slumped back into the sofa.

"You know, Gwen," said Lew, "I've been watching you and wondering if we shouldn't have you checked by a physician. I'm worried you could be going into shock."

"What makes you think that?"

"You have some of the symptoms."

"Like what?"

"Well, you're unusually calm, very precise in your movements, and that can mean—"

"No—I'm fine," said Gwen firmly. "I'm just… I'm doing my best to deal with all this. I mean, what good would screaming and crying do? Maybe later—when it hits me." She pressed her lips tight. "I do not need the emergency room."

"Okay, then," said Lew. "I hate to make things more difficult for you, but since your husband did not die of natural causes, we have work to do here—"

"I understand," said Gwen with a dismissive wave of one hand. "Do you need me to leave?"

"Yes, we'll have to secure the house and the property," said Lew. "But, Gwen, I may have more questions so I do have to ask that you remain here for the time being. Please don't touch anything until we've completed our investigation. That includes all the telephones, your computers, everything. Is that clear?"

"Certainly, but I'm surprised—well, I assume I can gather some overnight things?"

"Not yet, please. Now if you'll excuse me, I need to make a couple phone calls."

Ray picked up immediately. After telling him what had happened, Lew said, "I need photos before they move the body, Ray. You know the drill, and I'm sorry to call so late but if you can get over here— Good, thank you. Doc and I are both here. See you in a few minutes. No, I don't care how you get here, just get here."

"What's that all about?" Osborne said when she had finished.

"He's coming by canoe. Said it would be faster than driving."

"He's right about that," said Osborne. "Take him a good thirty minutes to drive it."

After calling the switchboard with instructions to have the officer on duty drive out to the Curry residence, Lew turned to Gwen. "Officer Martin will be here in about fifteen minutes. I'll have him drive you back into town and arrange for your stay at the inn.

"Now, Gwen, I realize this may be painful, but could you tell us exactly what happened after we left you and your husband at the Chamber offices?"

TWENTY-FIVE

GIVEN IT WAS LESS THAN two hours from when he had answered Lew's last question and finished packing the trunk for the job fair, Osborne could not accuse Hugh Curry of taking long to make a decision. According to Gwen, on arriving back at the Mirror Lake house, he had mixed himself a gin and tonic and walked down to the dock, where he sat watching the sunset and reading through his agenda and attendee list for the next day.

"Hugh loved having a cocktail on the dock before dinner. If it wasn't raining, he was down there every night. So I really didn't pay much attention. I was getting supper going and just assumed he was prepping for tomorrow," said Gwen. "He likes to open the job fairs by introducing all the participating firms, and since we have several new companies… Oh…" She paused. "I better call Anita Rasmussen and let the Chamber know they have to cancel—"

"I'll take care of it," said Lew. "Gwen, does the name Nora Loomis sound familiar?"

"Sure—that's the other woman who was murdered yesterday. Sounded awful, too. What is going on in this town, anyway?"

"How did *you* hear about it?" asked Lew.

"At the grocery store. I get all my news when I buy groceries."

"But the name doesn't ring a bell otherwise?"

"N-o-o. Wait—did she work at Universal Medical Supplies? They'd had a booth at every one of the job fairs and hired quite a few people. You know, I vaguely remember meeting someone named Nora. It's a lovely name. Could that have been Mrs. Loomis? And I remember Hugh assuring an older woman that all the personal information on the job fair applications was kept confidential. But, of course, now we know... My God, the man was desperate. Cracking up right in front of me and I had no idea." She brought both hands to her face and covered her mouth as her eyes widened in disbelief.

"Gwen, it's all speculation at this point but it doesn't look good," said Lew. "And I'm sorry to press you on these matters, but the sooner we can resolve things, the sooner you can get on with your life."

Gwen nodded. "You're right. I appreciate your concern. But o-o-h...my...God." Eyes shut tight, she shook her head back and forth.

"So take us back to what you were saying a minute ago. Your husband was down on the dock with his drink..."

"Right. For about a half hour or so. Then he walked in here and said to call him when supper was ready, that he would be in the office. Maybe that's when he wrote the note?" She looked at Lew and Osborne as if they had the answer.

"Next thing I know I'm setting the table and I hear a gun go off." Lips pressed tight as if to keep from breaking down, Gwen continued to sit quite still, her eyes focused on Lew. "Wish I could say more." She gave a sigh that sounded like a hiccup.

Thinking it a good time to change the subject, Osborne said, "The computer in your office—is that the one that has the job fair database?"

"Yes, but why would you need that now?"

"Well, we don't know what questions are likely to come up, so we'll need access. Do you agree, Chief Ferris?"

"Absolutely. I have a young man from the Wausau Crime Lab who is experienced in retrieving data from hard drives. With his help we may be able to track what your husband did with the money from the banks."

"Oh." Gwen nodded in agreement. "The password is 'Choppy,' after my dog. Once you're in, you'll see a folder named Job Fairs and the database is in that file. But I run my business off that, too. So, I mean, are you telling me I can't use my own computer?"

"Afraid so. At least until we've checked it out." Lew's tone was kind but firm.

Gwen rolled her eyes in frustration. "I certainly hope you won't take any longer than necessary." Osborne was struck by the change in attitude. One minute the woman was deep into grief and horror—now she was bullying again. He couldn't help feeling some sympathy for the dead guy with the bloody shorts.

"Since you mentioned your dog, Gwen," said Lew, ignoring the comment, "will he be okay staying here tonight? The Loon Lake Inn does not allow animals and I can't let you have any of your vehicles until we've completed our search of the property."

"Sure, Choppy's been fed. The yard is fenced and

he's got his doghouse. But you'll let me in to feed him in the morning, won't you?"

"If you'll show us where the dog food is, we'll take care of Choppy until we're finished here. Now let's get your overnight things," said Lew, turning to face the door. "I just heard a car pull up and that should be Officer Martin. He'll take you into town and get you settled.

"Oh, one more thing," said Lew as she stood up and started toward the door. "We've learned that the person responsible for DeeDee's pregnancy is a man by the name of Bert Moriarty. He's acknowledged the fact. I thought you should know."

It was only a microsecond, but the expression that flashed across Gwen Curry's face startled Osborne: the fury, the hot eyes. He had seen that look before—in the mad eyes of a rabid raccoon. An instant later, her porcelain features were serene, composed. But Osborne knew what he had seen and Lew had missed it.

"But you told me she was carrying Hugh's child," said Gwen, her dark voice cracking.

"I told you she was pregnant," said Lew. "I didn't say by whom. Doesn't the news that your husband was not responsible make things a little easier?"

Gwen stared at the floor for a long moment. "I… I…" She shrugged. "What the hell difference does it make now?" Pushing herself up from the sofa, she said, "If I'm leaving, I'll need my medication from the refrigerator—I'm diabetic. That isn't a problem, is it?"

"Of course not."

Lew opened the door to let the young officer in. "Chief Ferris," he said, handing her a document, "here's that search warrant you wanted."

"First the autopsy and now a *search warrant?*" said Gwen from where she stood in front of the open refrigerator. "So you were on your way out here no matter what Hugh did?"

"Once I had the warrant, yes," said Lew. "We had enough documentation to justify a search that could help us prove that your husband was defrauding several local banks. If we can find those counterfeit checks…"

"Wow, looks like I was the only one who *didn't* know," said Gwen in a low, sad tone as she closed the refrigerator door with a gentle shove. "Guess I can go now, huh?"

THE BOGUS CHECKS were right where Hugh said they would be—in a plastic container shoved under the rear seat in the extended cab of his truck. Six firms, all of which had been participants in the job fairs, had had their checks expertly altered. Several driver's licenses were in the container, too, each one bearing a different name and address but always the same photo: a headshot of Hugh Curry. "Man, this guy was good," said Dan Wright when he examined them the next day.

Following Gwen's instructions, Lew found it easy to access the job fair database, though it did not appear to have been updated within the last week. "That's funny, Doc," said Lew as she scrolled down through the names. "I thought we heard Gwen tell her husband that she had updated the information."

"On the server," said Osborne, after checking his notes. "Is this computer the server?"

"I have no idea," said Lew.

"He-e-e-y," said a familiar voice in a low tone from

behind them. "Before I do what you need me to do, is it okay to make a small announcement? I mean, with all due respect to the dead." He raised his eyebrows as if expecting to be admonished. "May I give you a little piece of news that affects *you,* Chief?"

It was obvious Ray was excited about something but, shoulders hunched and two cameras hanging around his neck, he was trying his best to respect the situation.

"Cut to the chase, Ray," warned Lew. "Just be aware I'm not in the mood for Ringling Bros. and Barnum & Bailey."

"Just thought you might appreciate knowing… FawnCam…has launched operations…in the deer garden…of the famed Ferris farm. DVDs available shortly."

"Thank you, Ray, but forget the DVDs. I need photos and I need them ASAP," said Lew from where she sat in front of the computer. "We've kept the EMTs waiting too long as it is."

"Okay, okay, I'm on it. It's just that Mallory and I are pretty pleased everything is working so well."

Lew stood up and gave Ray a grateful grin. "Good. And, hey, I appreciate your getting over here so fast."

"Ray," said Osborne, surprised, "how on earth did you find time *today* to set up FawnCam?"

"Only took an hour."

"What—the deer let you walk right up and hang a camera around their necks? They didn't run off?"

"Doc," Lew warned as she pointed toward the master bedroom, "you two can discuss this later."

"I'm going, I'm going," said Ray, even as he lingered half out the doorway. "The does were skittish but the young ones hesitated j-u-u-s-t long enough for me and Mallory to get three camcorders hung. Fact of the matter—" he raised an instructive index finger "—they love that deer garden, Chief. That's what made it easy. So easy that we may…have to pay *you* a commission."

One of the EMTs poked his head into the office. "We can't wait much longer, Chief Ferris. Could have another call any minute."

"Right. Ray, here's what I need—" Lew ripped a page from her notebook. "I made a list."

Ray gave it a quick glance and said, "You want me to shoot both color and black-and-white, right? Like I keep telling you—shouldn't you fire Pecore and put the good doc and myself on full-time? Right, Doc?"

"I hear you, Ray, but you and a full-time job—that's an oxymoron."

"Are you calling me a moron?"

"C'mon. I'm too tired for this," said Lew, taking him by the arm and walking him down the hall toward the master bedroom. As she gave him a gentle shove into the room, she said, "So when you've finished in the bathroom, be sure to get shots of all the rooms in this house. Place is a mess, I know, but we've got more than a suicide that happened here."

HALF AN HOUR LATER, Lew pushed her chair back from the Currys' computer and, yawning, said, "Doc, let's tackle this tomorrow. I am just exhausted. You must be, too." She looked up at him with a smile despite the fatigue in her eyes.

"Yes, I certainly am, sweetheart," said Osborne, pulling off the nitrile gloves he'd been wearing as he sorted through papers and debris. Standing behind her, he reached down to give her shoulders a gentle squeeze. "It's been a long day and getting through the mess in this place is going to take a while."

"You bet it is," said Lew, reaching for his hand and pressing it against her cheek.

A cursory search of the papers strewn through the office and the living room along with a scan of the folders on the computer desktop had yielded no hint of where Hugh Curry had stashed the money from the banks. "It's looking like we'll need Gwen's help to locate their financial records—unless they're all in that garbage bag." She pointed to the shredder.

"Funny we haven't found Curry's wallet," said Osborne. "I don't know any man who doesn't carry a wallet."

"I checked all those dressers in their bedroom and spent a little time sifting through the mess in the living room and kitchen areas," said Lew. "We'll have fresh eyes tomorrow." She turned to stare at the computer screen one last time, then shrugged. "At least Dan Wright knows computers. If anyone can find electronic financial files, it's that guy."

"Stay at my place tonight?" said Osborne, bending to nuzzle her ear.

Lew leaned into him. "No, no. Sounds tempting but I am in desperate need of a good night's sleep." She spun the chair around to face him. "And you know I'm not comfortable at your place when your daughter's there. I just feel…self-conscious. Y'know?"

"Like we're too old to be doing what we're doing?"

She laughed. "Maybe this weekend? My place? With

the way things are going, I may actually get to take the entire weekend off." She gave him a quick kiss, then headed down the hall to see how Ray was doing.

IT WAS AFTER MIDNIGHT when Lew and Osborne found themselves strolling across the yard toward the dock with Ray. The air was warm, the water glass; not a whisper of a breeze. And the sky so clear they could see the Milky Way, an ethereal scarf wending through millions of stars. A crescent moon cast a sword of light across the still surface of the lake and muted voices drifted from lighted windows on the opposite shore.

"I drew a map of where I found DeeDee's shoe and those two teeth. It's with the report I left in your office," said Ray as he slipped his cameras into a waterproof case before setting them carefully into the canoe. "The teeth are in an evidence bag on your kitchen counter, Doc."

"Good," said Osborne. "Lew, it's a formality at this point but I'll get DeeDee's dental records in the morning for an official confirmation. Here, Ray, let me give you a push." With a shove from Osborne, the canoe slipped into the water.

"'Night, you two," said Ray, his paddle making a soft "swoosh" as the canoe cleared the front of the dock. Pulling deep, he stopped. "Whoa, hold on. Can't believe there's a rock here. What the hell?" The paddle high in his left hand, he reached down with his right.

"Ouch! Something very sharp… Chief, Doc—let's get some light on this before someone gets hurt."

Within minutes, they were staring through the crystal-clear water of Mirror Lake. "Well, folks," said Ray, "your guess is as good as mine. Animal? Vegetable? Mineral? Or…one beat-up computer."

"Hey, look over there," said Lew, waving her flashlight across tiny slivers of leather and plastic floating close to the shore.

"I've got a net if you want to grab some of that," said Ray. Osborne took it from him and waded in a short way to scoop up the bits and pieces. Lew shone the flashlight over the contents, then said, "Gentlemen, I'm willing to bet this is all we'll find of Hugh Curry's wallet. I guess we'll be relying entirely on Mrs. Curry for purposes of identification."

"And personal financial records perhaps?" added Osborne, thinking of all the minutia a person's wallet might contain—details they might want kept secret from surviving family members.

WALKING BACK TO THE CRUISER after making sure the house was locked up, Lew said, "Doc, what do you think Gwen was making for supper?"

"I don't know—hadn't thought about it."

"I have."

"And?" He linked his arm through hers.

"And I saw nothing close to a meal being prepared on the stove or on the counters. Nothing in the sink that hadn't been there for weeks, if not months. And no table setting— though that would be hard to tell through all the mess."

"Boy, that never occurred to me," said Osborne. "You're right. Be interesting to hear what her answer will be to that, Lew." He watched her reach to open the door of the cruiser. Moonlight got caught in the curls falling over her forehead and gleamed off the irises of her dark, dark eyes. Osborne couldn't help it, he started planning for the weekend.

TWENTY-SIX

MALLORY WAS STILL UP and working away on her laptop as Osborne walked into the den. Setting his black bag off to one side, he said, "Honey, do you know how late it is?"

"Yeah, I do—but I want to get this done," said Mallory without taking her eyes off the computer screen. "Say, Dad—" she paused to look up at him with a wide grin "—guess what? I've decided to move in with you and run this FawnCam business for Ray."

At the expression on his face, she laughed out loud. "I am just *kidding.* For heaven's sake. But, seriously, I do think Ray is onto something this time. I've had e-mails back from the Smithsonian shops, two gun catalogs and the Outdoors Network." She turned back to her computer screen. "Two more e-mails and I'm done here."

"That's great, Mal," said Osborne, suddenly remembering Gretel, her guns and Ray's obvious crush on the woman. How would that fit with FawnCam? Would Ray dating Gretel upset Mallory?

"I'll head back to Evanston on Saturday, Dad. Ray and I are going to fish fry Friday night after we wrap up what he needs to do to keep everything moving forward."

"Um…you sure about that?"

"Yeah, why?" She turned around to look at him.

"Well, I think that Ray might have other plans is all. Might want to check with him." Osborne decided right then and there that *he* was not going to be the one to tell her.

"Oh, you mean the woman with the guns? He's pretty excited about Gretel. She can get us into even more markets through the companies she reps."

"Oh, that's good…I guess."

"Dad, what's wrong?" Mallory's eyes teased him. "You got something on your mind?"

"No."

"Yes, you do. I can see it. Oh, I know—I've stayed too long, haven't I?"

"Absolutely not. I love having you here."

"Dad, I've been through enough therapy to know *you* do not handle confrontation well. Now if you don't level with me, I'm going to insist you go back into rehab."

"All right, all right." Osborne gave up. "It's Ray, honey. The blonde. That Gretel woman with the guns. I think he's like…"

"Okay, Dad, here's the deal. First, let me turn off the computer." She hit a key, then waved a hand at him. "Sit down, would you please?"

Osborne plunked himself into the leather armchair that he had rescued from his office over Mary Lee's objections that it was too worn and ripped along the seat cushion. It was still ripped and worn *and* the most comfortable chair in the house.

"I know you think I'm in love with Ray, but I've learned a lot about him in the last few days. He's a wonderful guy, Dad, but I can never marry someone who can't read a spreadsheet."

"He can't read a spreadsheet?" Osborne stalled, wondering why that would be a problem. The guy had other qualities, after all.

"Hell, no. Numbers drive him nuts. But that doesn't mean he isn't fun."

"So what about Gretel? If he's attracted to her—that doesn't bother you?"

"D-a-a-d, I know the guy. When it comes to women, he is totally morally flexible. Always has been. You think I don't know that?" She angled her head with that teasing smile again. "That's part of what makes him a hell of a lot more interesting than most of the guys I date."

"Okay, then. I guess I'm not going to worry about you."

"I'm a big girl, Dad. Please…do not worry about me. Although…" she hesitated "…there is something." Osborne waited.

"Very likely, I won't marry again. I mean, I don't *want* to get married again."

"Have you been talking to Lew?"

"I'm serious, Dad, because I worry about you— would you be okay with that? I have so many things I want to do and I'm not big on having kids. Erin's kids feel like they're mine, too, and I love that. But I worry that you'll think I'm… I worry that you'll worry."

"Oh, Mal, come here," said Osborne, standing up and opening his arms. Mallory got to her feet and walked into his embrace. He held her close. "I just want you to be happy. If you're happy with your career and your friends—that's fine with me." He tipped her face so he could look into her eyes and said, "You know…you've grown up to be a very different woman from your mother. And that's good because life is different for women these days."

"Thank you. I needed to hear that, Dad."

She pulled away and Osborne started for the door. "Just one question, kiddo. What's an SBF? I heard you and Erin talking about that."

"Oh, jeez, Dad! It means Secret Boy Friend. Like the guy who's totally off-limits but you have a crush on him anyway."

"Don't tell me Erin has an SBF."

"No! She's very happy with Mark. We were talking about me. If you have to know—referring to Ray. But, Dad, that was so yesterday. Things have changed."

"The spreadsheet."

"Right. The spreadsheet."

Osborne slowly walked toward his bedroom. What was it Mallory had said? Morally flexible…makes him fun… Jeez, Louise! Would he ever understand women?

HE WAS STILL HALF AWAKE when he heard the bedroom door creak open. A creature, its fur standing on end, loomed in the shadows. Wavering on hind legs, it crept toward the bed. The eyes were hot and angry. The talons dripped blood. As it came at him, he knew: Lew was next.

Osborne screamed—and screamed again but the cries never left his throat. He woke with a thud to a long, slow snore from Mike. Blinking, he sat up. The bedroom door stood slightly ajar—just as he'd left it. Through the open window he heard the hoot of an owl. A west wind moaned through the pines. His world was unchanged except for those eyes—he knew they had been there.

TWENTY-SEVEN

OSBORNE WOKE TO a chorus of crows, woodpeckers, robins and finches arguing international politics. Bright sunshine did nothing to curb their enthusiasm but it did encourage him to leap out of bed and head for the kitchen, where he found that Mallory had already put the coffeepot on to brew.

A full mug of coffee in hand and Mike bounding beside him, he headed down the stone stairway to the dock. Inhaling summer with all its sounds and warm breezes and his own pleasure in being alive, he paused at the end of the dock, took a deep sip of his coffee and studied the lake. A good walleye chop beckoned. He glanced down the shoreline to his right. Ray's boat was out. Of course.

He had promised Lew that he would stop by the Curry place at ten. If Dan hadn't made it up from Wausau, the plan was for Osborne to load the wrecked computer into his car and drive it down to the crime lab.

"Hey, Mike," he called to the dog who was busy retrieving the stick he had tossed out over the waves. "C'mon, let's see what the chief wants. I have a hunch I should pack my waders. You know, if all goes well, this could be one fine day for the float tube." But even as he said that, he winced.

Float-tube fishing was tough. Lew loved it but he still hadn't figured out how to maneuver his way onto the water without looking like a wounded elephant; kick out to a good spot without asking Lew to stop and wait for him six times; tie on a trout fly bearing some resemblance to the insects hatching around him; and, finally, execute backcasts, forward casts and power snaps—all without being sabotaged by leg cramps. He was close to mastering everything but the leg cramps. But, hey, whatever it cost to fly fish with Lewellyn. He could fish through pain.

"I saw it in her eyes all day yesterday," said Osborne, trusting Mike to give him good advice. "That woman has got to get on water soon. The endorphins are calling. Runners need to run, bikers need to bike and fishermen need to fish. I tell you, Mike—" Osborne pointed a finger of authority at the dog "—as Ted Williams used to say, 'Every day you fish adds a day to your life.'" Mike yelped agreement as Osborne tossed him not one but two doggie treats.

AN HOUR LATER HE WAS humming his way toward the Curry place, past fields of grass buttered gold by the sun, lush-leaved potato fields and public landings crammed with boat trailers starting the weekend early. He parked near the cluster of police cars and a van that filled the driveway as well as the road in front of the Curry house. He wasn't surprised. Before leaving home, he'd made a quick call to Marlene who said he would find Lew here with three of the Wausau boys, including Dan.

"They were on the road at seven this morning," Marlene had said. "You got banks losing money and they're all over the place, doncha know. Not like some crumb bum gets knifed at a tavern—then they could care less. Say, Doc, did you hear what Ray saw out at Chief Ferris's place last night?"

"Out there or on that FawnCam of his?"

"Yeah, on the video. Y'know that thing really works. The chief thought she had a mountain lion—no way. It's a wolf! Huge, too, Ray said."

"You're kidding."

"No, I'm not. Those fawns may not be long for this world." Marlene paused. "Do you think that wolf would eat those camcorders that Ray hung around their necks?"

"Don't know, Marlene. My dog did a good job on a remote control."

OSBORNE FOUND LEW on her knees just inside the open front door. "Get a load of this, Doc," she said, pointing to a colorful box that had been pulled out of the larger box in which it had been shipped. "A karoke machine— professional model. Now what on earth could the Currys have planned to do with that?"

"Train for *American Idol?*" said Osborne, thinking of the plastic version that Erin had bought for his grand-children. They had had great fun with it until someone left the microphones out in the rain.

"Well, I can't imagine…" said Lew as Osborne extended a hand to help her to stand up. The day was already heating up and with no air-conditioning, the temperature in the house, even with all the doors and windows open, was nearing eighty degrees—enough to leave a sheen of perspiration across Lew's forehead.

Didn't seem to bother her, however. Dusting grit from the floor off her hands, she looked fresh and rested.

"On the way out I stopped by Dr. Elman's office with those teeth that Ray found at the Moccasin Lake site. Marcy had said he was DeeDee's dentist. Elman promised to pull her chart and have a report for you early this afternoon."

"Well, not much to do here, Doc. That damaged computer doesn't need to go down to Wausau after all. Dan could tell right away that it is all that's left of the server that Hugh Curry was using—and the hard drive was completely destroyed. The updated database, any financial records that Hugh may have kept on the server's hard drive, he obliterated with a sledgehammer and finished off with a good drowning. No one'll ever find those records. So there is no hope of using that to tell us where or what Hugh did with all his money. In the meantime, because it's bank fraud, the Feds have directed Wausau to take over the search here at the house and in the office Hugh was using at the Chamber."

"That must mean you have the day off," said Osborne, his heart lifting.

"Not so fast, kiddo." She punched him lightly in the shoulder. "I have phone calls to return and a small mountain of paperwork to finish up."

"Even with Hugh Curry's confession and the fact his wife is pretty sure he was familiar with Nora Loomis and had chosen her as one of his easy marks?"

"I wish it were that easy. But I am putting the homicide investigation on hold until I see what they find here at the house." Lew set the karaoke box back in its shipping container. She cut her eyes sideways toward Osborne as she spoke, her voice low and teasing. "So, Doc, did I tell you Ralph Steadman left me a message yesterday…"

His heart sank. Steadman, owner of Ralph's Sporting Goods and a guy who was definitely "morally flexible" when it came to his marriage, had the bad habit of hitting on Lew, which irritated the hell out of Osborne. That plus the jerk's talent for launching arcane discussions of fly-fishing that Lew appreciated but were way, w-a-a-y over Osborne's head. Knowing Steadman did it just to intimidate him, Osborne despised the razzbonya.

And so he half listened, eyes cast down. Very likely Lew was trying to let him down easy with the news that she had been invited to fish with Ralph and some visiting bigwigs from Orvis or St. Croix or Cabela's or BassPro…

"Doc—" Lew waved a hand in front of his face "—are you listening to me? Ralph said he got in some new kayaks that have been rigged for fly-fishing and wants me to try one out. But I told him I need two—not one. And he agreed! I know he's figuring we'll end up buying 'em."

"Any strings attached?" said Osborne, unwilling to believe his good luck.

"Only that I can't afford to go very far in case we have new developments on this Curry situation or something else goes haywire. So I was thinking we'd start out on Big Pine Lake, just north of here where I'll still have cell service. I've been told there's a creek that runs parallel to the Gudegast down into the Loon Lake chain. I've never tried it but it could have brookies, maybe even browns. Would you be up for that? Do some exploring?"

"How soon can I pick up the kayaks?"

"Not necessary," said Lew with a chuckle as she leaned up to kiss his cheek. "I got 'em this morning. See you 'round five."

TWENTY-EIGHT

"ON A LAKE THIS BIG, we should use streamers," said Lew, leaning over the tailgate of her truck to reach for one of her small plastic cases of trout flies. "But these winds aren't going to make it easy." She squinted into the east, her face against the wind. "What do you think—gusting twenty, thirty miles an hour, Doc?"

"I'd say so. But it has to be over ninety degrees, Lew. At least the wind takes the edge off."

Osborne watched as she opened a box of sparkling, colorful trout flies—fatter and longer than any he'd fished with so far. "In the lake, it'll be all about bass and pike—maybe even a muskie, Doc."

"Does it make a difference that Big Pine is deep with dark water?"

"Oh, yeah, means the fish can stay cool in the heat. Plus they'll see a lot more minnows and crayfish than they will insects. See this?" She pulled out a steamer with a bright yellow body. "Let's start you with a Muddler Minnow."

"What about you?" said Osborne, picking up his fly rod, which he had managed to rig a little faster this time. Lew was always way ahead of him. The minute she got close to water she was a speed demon, whether pulling on waders in a split second or rigging her fly rod. He was always at least ten minutes behind.

But today, with no waders needed in the kayaks and his fingers becoming more adept each time he rigged his rod, Osborne cut five minutes off his time.

"I'm going to try a Conehead Madonna—the trout fly that Marcy Kurlander's father tied for DeeDee. It's similar to your Muddler, Doc."

"Why can't I try one, too?" The trout fly that she was pinning to the patch of lamb's wool on her fly-fishing vest was too gorgeous to resist.

"I only have one. We'll trade off later if you want."

BEFORE GETTING INTO the kayak, which held a rack for his fly rod along one side, Osborne waved to Lew, who was pushing her kayak into the water. "One question. If we're planning to be on the lake for a while and then head down that creek, are there any rapids to worry about?"

"Oh, gosh, no, Doc. The guy who told me about it said he kayaked it last fall and it was easygoing."

"Okay, then I'm not going to worry about anything getting too wet," said Osborne.

Rushing up to the truck, he grabbed a sweatshirt. If they were going to be on the water for hours in this wind, it might cool down later. He also tucked his reading glasses into his shirt pocket instead of zippering them into the fly-fishing vest. And at the last minute, he grabbed his camera.

Then he put his life jacket on the seat of the kayak to cushion it, shoved his fishing vest down into the front of the kayak, pushed the boat onto the water, straddled the set and plopped in. The lake was choppy with waves but the kayaks were sturdy and flat and cut through the chop with ease.

Lew led the way to a small bay. There she set her paddle aside and reached for her fly rod. Her instructions were simple. "You want to show these fish a disoriented minnow, Doc. So first angle your kayak to have the wind behind you. Then watch for the gusts. Time your backcast to coincide with the end of the gust—then make your forward cast so you present your fly in the calm behind the gust. Got it?"

"Oh yeah." Osborne waited as the wind buffeted. Then, at what he thought was the tail end of a gust, he raised his fly rod and backcast with a power snap, only to hear Lew shout, "Duck!" He did, barely avoiding hooking himself in the head.

Lew was laughing. "You'll get the hang of it. The good thing is we're only twenty minutes from the hospital—and they got a whole wing dedicated to hook removal, doncha know."

"Very funny," said Osborne, raising his rod again. He was determined to make this work. He waited. A gust blew hard from directly behind, then eased off. Raising his right arm, Osborne launched a backcast, only to have the line snapped up, whipped around and spit out by a monster of a crosswind. Fly line, leader, tippet and trout fly spun crazily until all ended up in a massive knot, a knot so dense it would take days, possibly months, even years to unravel. Osborne stared at it. A lot of words came to mind—every one challenging him to be morally flexible.

THEY FOUND SHELTER from the wind just past the opening to the creek. Sitting on a hummock under a stand of young balsam, Lew worked at his knot while Osborne set out wedges of cheddar cheese and crackers. She hadn't had the easiest time casting either, though she hadn't destroyed her equipment. And so they made the decision to give up on Big Pine and head for quieter water.

"Tell you what, Doc," said Lew, clipping away and digging deep into various pockets on her fly-fishing vest. "I've got the fly line okay and we'll just tie on a new leader and some tippet. Forget the rest of this."

"What about the Muddler?"

"We'll sacrifice it. Not the first trout fly you've lost." She grinned in sympathy, then reached for one of the crackers he'd prepared. "Something I forgot to tell you earlier, by the way. While the Wausau boys were getting started on the Curry place this morning, I happened to check the refrigerator and took a good look at Gwen Curry's supply of medication since she didn't take all of it with her when she left last night. Turns out she mail-orders from Universal Medical Supplies."

"That's interesting," said Osborne.

"I thought so. I called Rick Meyerdierk and asked him to check the dates on her recent orders, and if those orders were called in."

"You're thinking of Nora Loomis?"

"Um-hmm. I'm remembering the unmistakable sound of a shredder and that Nora thought she heard a couple fighting. What if Gwen is lying? What if she knew all along that her husband was a little too interested in DeeDee? What if what Nora overheard was Hugh confessing to Gwen that he had killed DeeDee and it was the fight that followed that was on that tape?"

"Which would make Gwen an accomplice."

"Certainly changes things. I just… I don't trust the

woman. So maybe I'm being ornery because I don't want to make it easy for her. Does that make me a bad person?" Lew gave a sheepish grin.

"I wouldn't feel bad about it if I were you," said Osborne. "Better to have every question answered, every possibility examined. You're not being ornery, you're doing your job, Lewellyn." She kissed him.

THEY PUSHED THE KAYAKS BACK into the stream. A slight current carried them forward and the tamaracks lining the bank, their roots happy in the wetland border, provided good cover from the wind. Whether it was the wind that had fine-tuned his casting skills, Lew's kiss or the new leader and tippet along with his favorite dry fly (an Adams Wulff Size 10), Osborne wasn't sure— but to his surprise he could make his fly go right where he wanted it to. No belly in the line this time and a silent, delicate presentation of his trout fly.

And then, in a small, quiet pocket of water less than a quarter mile downstream, he made another discovery: the biggest fish were in the least likely spot. Not only did he set the hook on a nine-inch brookie, he followed that success with a stunning twenty-one-inch brown trout! Lew, pleased for him, refused to let him release the fish before she could take a photo.

As she handed the camera back, he heard a sound off in the distance—familiar but unexpected. A low rumble, it added to the pleasant haze of the summer evening. Even the temperature was easing off. "Whaddya think that noise is, Lew?" he asked, not taking his eyes from the trout fly he was mending with short, quick flicks of his rod. Never had he felt so at one with the world around him: water, fly rod, trout fly and the woman in the kayak ahead. Life doesn't get much better than this, he was thinking as she answered.

"Not sure, Doc," said Lew, her voice happy as she set the hook on a ten-inch brook trout. "I was told there were no rapids in here." Unworried, they let the kayaks drift and kept casting. The lake may have been a disappointment but this creek was rich with fish. For a while, neither of them noticed that the rumble was growing closer.

TWENTY-NINE

OSBORNE WAS SO PLEASED with his tight fly line and so focused on mending the Adams Wulff dry fly across the riffles and eddies in the stream that he didn't notice his kayak was picking up speed. The wind, though rebuffed by the tamaracks bordering the stream, found plenty of opportunity to roar high overhead and mask the sound of distant waters.

Neither Lew nor Osborne heard the rapids until they rounded a bend. Just five hundred feet ahead the stream split around an island of exposed rock ringed with half-submerged boulders. From a distance, the narrow chutes on each side of the outcropping appeared to drop maybe six inches or so. Osborne wasn't worried. He'd canoed Class Three rapids, which made these look easy.

"My guess is a foot drop at the most, Doc," said Lew. "Shouldn't be bad—" Before she finished speaking, her kayak took on a life of its own, leaping into the swirling waters. "Watch your fly rod through the chutes," she cried. "Try to keep it out of those branches!"

"I will—don't worry, Lew," shouted Osborne over the water, which now roared louder than the wind. "Uh-oh." In slow motion he watched the front of Lew's kayak tip up, up and over. An instant later, he hit the same hidden rock, the bow of his kayak airborne for a split second then tipping sideways, spilling him into the rushing water.

The current was hard and fast, pounding. This is not good, he thought. At first the water seemed about two feet deep and he was buffered as he held tight to the back end of the kayak—but the water level changed and the current slammed him onto sharp, rough rocks. The kayak righted itself but it was fast filling with water. Osborne slammed his fly rod into the boat and grabbed on with both hands.

The pounding on his lower body and legs was severe, and all he could think was, when is this going to stop? I think I might die…

As his head hit a rock, light exploded, blinding his eyes. I'm dead…no, not yet. He drifted into semiconsciousness. Time slowed. He hung on, waiting to feel his bones break—they would if he didn't find deeper water. The bank! He had to get to the bank. Out of her merciless current.

One slippery toehold after another, he forced his way off to the left, out of the water pulling him through the minefield of river rock. All of a sudden the water was up to his chest and he was struggling to gain a footing when he saw his life jacket, his fishing vest and his sweatshirt float from the kayak. He reached into the kayak and grabbed for his camera only to let it drop as his glasses floated by. He lunged for those instead. Glasses in one hand, he reached out again for the camera. In that second, his kayak was swept back into the stream and on its way without him.

"Lew!" Osborne scanned the bank ahead to see if she'd made it. No sign of her. He took a deep breath, felt for broken bones. Then, grabbing one tag alder branch after another, he pulled himself through the deep holes along the bank and around a bend. The stream bed gave way to a shallow, sandy bottom, making it possible for him to haul himself up and around until he could see downstream.

On the opposite bank was a dry, sandy stretch of shoreline. Lew lay there, facedown, not moving. Breathing hard, Osborne's voice croaked as he called out, "Are you okay? Lew?"

She raised her head slightly. He pushed himself to his knees, thankful he could get that far, then onto his feet. Determined not to fall and be dragged again, he staggered across the shallow, rushing water on shaky legs. As he bent over Lew, she pushed herself up onto her elbows, a grimace of pain on her face. "Doc, are you okay?"

"I have no goddamn idea. I'm alive, I'm upright. What about you? Is anything broken?"

"Not sure. Just…no…strength." She pulled herself sideways and lowered her head onto the sand. "I need to catch my breath."

"Lie still." He ran his hands down her limbs, feeling for trouble. The fishing shorts and sandals made it easy to see and palpate long, red scrapes running from her knees to her ankles. "No bones broken, Lew. But we're both very badly bruised."

"Let me try getting up, Doc," said Lew, bracing herself on her arms and pushing up onto her knees.

"Take it easy, sweetheart." Osborne dropped onto the ground beside her. "Let's just sit still for a few minutes. I'm exhausted."

"Wait'll I talk to the sonofabitch who told me this

was calm water," said Lew, pushing her wet hair back from her face. "Man, I am so pissed. Our kayaks are gone—what about your fly rod?"

"Last I saw it was in the kayak, but then everything else I had in there was dumped. I don't know but I couldn't hold on. What about you?"

"Me neither. And I made the big mistake of taking my fishing vest off when we were on the lake, so that's gone along with my cell phone and everything. But the hell with all that. Jeez, Doc, I thought for a minute there I was going to get us both killed. I mean, really, we're lucky our skulls weren't fractured on those rocks."

"I have to say that crossed my mind, too." They looked at each other and burst into laughter. Long, hard, semi-hysterical laughter.

Finally Lew wiped the tears from her eyes, wriggled her toes as she dumped the sand from her sandals and said, "So where the hell do we go from here?"

"Well…" Osborne got to his feet and reached out his hand. "Depends on whether or not you can stand up."

"I'll try. I have to say, laughing made me feel better." She got to her knees first, then onto one foot and the other. "I think I got it." She smiled. "But, man, am I banged up. I hurt!"

"We'll feel worse tomorrow," said Osborne. "Look, the sun is in the west and I know from the Gazetteer that this creek runs parallel to the channel to Mirror Lake— the one Mason calls "the secret passage"—so I think we ford the stream here where it's shallow and head due south. We're bound to run into the channel and, if we have to, we'll *swim* up to Mirror Lake."

"Darn," said Lew, "if it weren't for all the wetlands back in here, we'd have a shot at a logging road."

AFTER FORDING THE STREAM, they pushed through a wall of young popple, which gave way to a shadowed ravine guarded by old hemlocks and much easier to walk. The canopy of ancient trees had long blotted out the sun, so there was little overgrowth on the forest floor. Soon they were facing the edge of a swampy stretch of tamarack and black spruce. Osborne's watch had stopped working but he figured they had at least another hour or more of light.

Spotting a berm that was less forested, they decided to detour slightly in order to pull themselves up onto it. "Whoa, what is this?" said Lew, once they were standing on top. "Looks like we found an old logging lane after all."

"Sure does. Someone's been in here recently, too," said Osborne. "What do you think—do we continue toward the channel or reverse to see where this old road leads?"

"Let's keep straight. We know the channel can't be far. But a road like this could wind back a couple miles at least. I'd just as soon find a place that's familiar."

"I agree. Chances are excellent we'll see some kayakers on the channel who can help us out."

They headed southwest, relieved to have an easier path. They hadn't been walking five minutes when the logging lane came to an abrupt end at the back of an old barn. From the outside, the barn looked abandoned—the wood weathered a deep gray and windows shuttered.

Walking around to the front of the building, they

found a footpath that twisted its way through a cedar swamp of slash and tamarack, then down a steep bank to water: the channel to Mirror Lake. "Hey, Doc, we did it," said Lew, standing on the bank. "And look—" she pointed to where grasses growing along the shore had been crushed "—someone's been pulling a boat in and out of here. Maybe we can hitch a ride?"

"Lew, I'm going to see what's in that barn back there. You never know—could be an old fishing boat stored in there."

"Yep, worth a peek. I'll keep watch here in case somebody comes by."

One push at the old door at the front of the barn and it swung open. To Osborne's surprise, a full half of the interior was filled with brand-new packaged goods—the boxes resplendent with colorful replicas of their contents and stacked carefully one on top of the other. The remaining space was packed with wooden crates and flattened cardboard shipping containers. An old wooden worktable running along one wall held spools of packing tape, tools and sorted stacks of shipping labels.

Osborne stepped outside. "Lew, get up here," he hollered. "You won't believe what's in this place."

"Better be good," said Lew as she walked up from the water, "'cause I don't want to walk any more than I absolutely have to." He held the door for her to walk in. "Oh!"

Together they walked down the center of the barn, amazed at the contents of the boxes. "Look at this," said Osborne, waving an arm. "Dozens of computers, boxes and boxes of iPods... Just look at all these video games, Lew. And here—flat-screen TVs. This place is packed with electronics! Thousands of dollars' worth."

"*Tens* of thousands of dollars' worth—a warehouse of electronic toys! Stuck out in the middle of nowhere. Can you imagine a kid walking in here—"

"I think they have—I'll bet you anything Mason has been here. She's been telling everyone about the hidden treasure she found kayaking up the Secret Passage."

"HONEST TO PETE," said Lew, hands on her hips and shaking her head as she looked around. "Why would someone want to store their merchandise way out here? And who owns this place, I wonder?"

"I vaguely remember a proposal submitted to the town board a couple years ago," said Osborne. "An elderly woman from Milwaukee who inherited a chunk of property in this area had the crazy idea of building a shopping mall right along the channel here. The idea was absurd, of course—the wetlands surrounding this small peninsula are not buildable and the town board was not going to allow her to bring in fill. Looks to me like she found a use for her property after all."

"Or maybe she rents it out," said Lew. "Take a look, Dr. Osborne." She pointed at an opened cardboard box that had been set down near the door. The address on the label read: Gwen Curry; 5317 Mirror Lake Road; Loon Lake, Wisconsin 54545.

"Gwen Curry? This must be her eBay operation," said Osborne.

"And these must be her cell phones," said Lew, pointing to a stack of boxed phones. "And prepaid phone cards, too. Tidy operation." An unboxed phone lay next to the stack, its charger plugged into an outlet on the worktable. Lew picked it up and reached for one of the phone cards. "I'm going to call for help first, then we'll try Mrs. Curry."

LEW WAS PUNCHING IN the nonemergency number of the Loon Lake Police switchboard when Osborne saw a bright flash at the window and heard a rustling outside the open barn door. Walking over to the window, he peered out but an overgrown bush obscured the view. He stepped outside only to see a flicker of something dark disappear down the path leading to the water. A deer? Maybe a bear? A mother and two cubs had been sighted in the area.

Curious as to what he had seen, Osborne decided to chance running into a bear. Alert to any sign of the sow, he followed the path to the bank only to catch sight of a lone canoe heading off toward a far bend in the channel. The sun was so low all he could see was a silhouette.

Though the canoe was already a good hundred yards away, Osborne called out. Maybe it was the swish of paddle in water, maybe it was the evening breeze blowing in the opposite direction, but it was apparent that he wasn't heard. The dark figure in the canoe, its back to Osborne, rounded the bend and disappeared.

THIRTY

Friday morning arrived too soon. Osborne moved with care from the bed. Steady doses of ibuprofen had done little to relieve the soreness in his lower back and legs. He stretched, then stretched again. The first cup of coffee helped. He called Lew.

"How are *you* feeling this morning?" he said.

"Old. Very, very old, Doc. I may be in one piece but I am moving s-l-o-o-w. Just called Marlene. She patched me through to Dan Wright, who spent the night in town. He said they figure they have half a day to go before they've sorted through everything in that house—still no money or trace of it."

"And Gwen?"

"Dan said they are letting her in late this morning when they've finished. No one wants anything to do with that dog—it lunged at one of the guys trying to feed it yesterday. If I feel better this afternoon, I want to sit down and listen to that tape from Universal Medical again. Knowing Gwen ordered from there has changed my perspective on that. It's bugging me."

"Don't rush it, Lew. You got beat up pretty bad."

"How's your head, Doc? That's quite a bump you have."

"I iced it before I went to bed but it's sore. Lew, if

you feel better later, would you join me for fish fry this evening?"

"Can I get back to you on that? I'm taking the morning to make some calls from home and just take it easy for a while. My shins are black and blue from the knees down to my ankles."

"Mine, too."

"I called my friend over in the Department of Natural Resources who recommended that stream, and guess what?"

"We kayaked the wrong one?"

"No. He canoed it last summer when we were having that drought and the water was down. Said he had to portage five times. I am so sorry, I should have remembered that, Doc. We've had so much rain this spring and summer—"

"Lew, it was not your fault."

"I know but—"

"Lewellyn…" He affected the sternest tone in his repertoire, the one he'd used on people who refused to floss.

"Okay, Doc." He could hear her smiling. "Later."

IT WASN'T UNTIL THREE in the afternoon that the soreness eased and Osborne felt like he'd rejoined the living. He decided to stop by Lew's office and see if she had made it in. Marlene was on the switchboard and, as he entered, said, "Doc, have you been out to check on the chief? I left two messages in the last half hour and she hasn't called in. Tried her cell phone, too."

"That definitely won't work—it's at the bottom of the creek."

"Right—I forgot."

"My hunch is she took some ibuprofen and is getting a much-needed nap," said Osborne. "That's what worked for me. Are these urgent messages? Should I drive out there?"

"Oh, no, I just wanted her to know that the Wausau boys dropped off a preliminary report—that young Dan guy said they really didn't find anything more than the checks and the fake driver's licenses. He was going to stop by the Chamber and take a look at the equipment they have there. He thinks Curry may have been printing the checks there during off-hours. He also said he would be checking in with the pathologist doing the autopsy on Hugh Curry. Anything unusual, he'll leave a message on her voice mail. Otherwise he'll e-mail the report first thing Monday morning.

"Oh—and I wanted Chief Ferris to know that Ray stopped in this morning. He said he was in touch with a buddy of his who fishes that stream where it enters Loon Lake. The guy's got a flat-bottomed skiff that can make it up quite a ways. They're gonna see if they can maybe locate those kayaks."

"Ray does have his virtues," said Osborne. "You heard he was kind enough to canoe up and get us last night?"

"You think he needs much of an excuse to be in a boat?" Marlene winked. "Hey, Ray's got a heavy date tonight—that blonde from Duluth. My niece, Laura, who's been working the night switchboard, calls her 'sniper girl.'"

"You mean Gretel?"

"Yep, Gretel with the guns," said Marlene with a chuckle. Then her eyes turned serious. "You know she was in the Army and saw active duty in Afghanistan.

That's where she got her training and she sure knows her stuff. Laura's so impressed, I won't be surprised if she enlists. Ray better not fool around with that gal."

"Really? She was in the military?"

"You haven't been reading the news, Doc," said Marlene. "Today's Army is different from when you and I were growing up. I must have half a dozen friends and relatives with daughters who've enlisted—some are career military and love it."

"Guess I shouldn't be surprised," said Doc. "I've always known women to be better with shotguns, and Lew is no slouch with a handgun." Then he slapped a hand on the counter in front of the dispatch window. "Before I leave, I think I'll take care of something Chief Ferris and I have been puzzling over, Marlene. Would you have a minute to help me play that CD we got from Universal Medical Supplies—the phone call that Nora Loomis overheard?"

"If you don't mind waiting a few minutes, Doc. Laura's due in to relieve me. That way I won't have to worry about the switchboard."

SITTING ACROSS FROM each other in Lew's conference room, Marlene played the Universal Medical CD three times—twice for Osborne and a third time for herself. "That caller has quite a lisp, don't they?" said Marlene, tipping her head as she listened.

"Less a lisp than a defined sibilant 's' sound," said Osborne. "Distinctive, but the connection isn't good enough to get the full range of the voices. Darn. I thought I might hear more this time. Oh, well." He checked his watch. "Gosh, it's been a while. I'm beginning to worry that Lew feels worse than she told me she did."

Picking up the phone in the conference room, he tried Lew at home again, but no answer. "I'll wait an hour and try again, Marlene."

"You're right to worry, Doc. When she called in this morning I could tell she wasn't feeling great—and she's never willing to take it easy like a normal person, y'know."

"I would drive out there but you know what a private person she is, Marlene. I hate to go without calling ahead."

"I know what you mean," Marlene said with a nod.

Osborne checked his watch. He would wait just an hour and try Lew again.

THIRTY-ONE

OSBORNE HAD JUST DECIDED to stop by Erin's house, a block away, and wait there before trying Lew again, when Ray's smiling face appeared on the steps leading up to the entrance to the police department.

No tasteless T-shirts today. This was Ray in what he liked to call his "sua-vey" mode: trim black slacks—which Osborne guessed had to be brand-new since he'd never seen them before—and a crewneck, long-sleeved black pullover. Waving to Osborne, he held the door for Mallory and Gretel to enter.

"Doc! We've been looking for you," said Ray. "You've met Gretel, right?"

"Yes, indeed," said Osborne, shaking her hand. "And don't you look like the movie star, Mr. Pradt. So, Gretel, I understand these two have roped you into their business plan?"

"We'll see," said Gretel, with a light laugh. "I'm taking one of the DVDs back to Duluth to share with our sales team. It could fit with some of the hunting products that we carry in our consumer catalogs. I was telling Ray and Mallory that we sell night-vision-type camcorders that hunters can set up to watch the deer that come to their feeders during the night. FawnCam could be a natural addition to that line."

"And Marlene tells me you saw active duty?"

"I did," said Gretel. "Been back for a year now—"

"Hey, Gretel, that…reminds me," said Ray, interrupting. "What…do you do…if you miss your mother-in-law?"

"Oh, no," groaned Mallory. "Gretel, I warned you…"

"I don't know—what?" said Gretel.

"Reload. Try again."

"That's a pretty tasteless joke to tell someone like me," said Gretel. And she wasn't smiling.

Mallory caught Osborne's eye, not a little amused. A moment of awkward silence, then Ray raised both arms and said, "All right, all right—I know a lot of other people who've found that funny."

"It's just that when you've been in combat…" said Gretel. She gave a sad smile. "I wish I *could* find it funny."

"I'm sorry," said Ray. "I am—very, very sorry."

"It's okay," said Gretel. But it wasn't okay and they all knew it.

In a move to rescue Ray, Mallory piped up. "So, Dad, we've got the FawnCam all set up for you and Chief Ferris. We thought you two could follow us out to Ray's place and watch some of the video from yesterday and this morning. Got a couple of good views of the wolf."

"You're kidding," said Osborne. "And the fawns are still alive?"

"Alive and filming," said Ray.

"The views are from a distance," said Mallory. "You can see that the fawns are alongside the does waiting for the wolf to leave…"

"Ray, Mallory," said Gretel, "if I go with you two, is

my car safe parked on the street? I have a trunk full of…merchandise, you know?"

"Let's not take a chance," said Ray. "I'll drive with you. Mallory, Doc—meet you at my place?"

"You okay with all this?" Osborne asked his daughter as the door swung closed behind Ray and Gretel.

"Dad, give it up, will you? I am very okay. I understand why Ray's attracted to her—she's blond, she's pretty, and she can shoot better than he can. Of course, now that we know she has no sense of humor… Dad, what's wrong?" Mallory laid a hand on his arm. "You've got something on your mind."

"It's nothing. Lew and I hit some rapids and got tipped out of our kayaks last night. We're both limping today—and I haven't been able to reach her. Got a break in the homicide investigations that she needs to know about—"

"You want to try now before we get in our cars?"

Walking over to the counter in front of the switchboard, Osborne asked Laura to try Lew's home again. Still no answer. "All I get is voice mail," said Laura. "Want to leave a message?"

"Yes, let her know I'll be at Ray's in about seven minutes—and ask her to please call me as soon as she gets the message."

Osborne followed Mallory back toward Loon Lake Drive. Halfway there he almost turned back, thinking it might not be a bad idea to drive by Lew's place after all. He had the excuse of making sure she felt up for fish fry with everyone. But he decided to wait one more half hour. He needed to stop by the house to change clothes before going to dinner anyway. If she didn't answer by five-thirty, he would definitely drive out to the farm.

RAY HAD RIGGED UP the video monitor so everyone sitting around his kitchen table could get a good view. "So let's check out what's happening right now," he said, pushing a button on a remote control. The trunks of pine trees came into view and the camera moved slowly, slowly toward one. Then it stopped, looked around and moved toward more trunks.

"This isn't real exciting, Ray," said Mallory. "Show them the wolf."

"All right." He hit another button. "The best way to do this is to rewind to interesting sections." Osborne felt his patience in short supply as he watched a lot of tree trunks, a path through more trees, a long pause down by the small lake that fronted Lew's farmhouse and, finally, an approach to the deer garden. "Over there!" said Mallory, pointing at a dark shape along one edge of the garden. "See the wolf?"

Everyone leaned forward, intent on the shape as it loped along. Then it was gone.

"Ray," said Mallory, "can you play the film from half an hour ago? I thought I saw the wolf just as we were leaving to come into town—see if you can find that sequence." The film spun back then forward, minutes turned into mini-seconds.

"Wait! Back up," said Osborne. "What was that?"

"Looks like a person," said Gretel, leaning forward. Ray backed the tape up and ran it in real time. The phone rang suddenly. Ray hit Pause then reached for the phone on the counter. Waiting for Ray to get rid of the caller, it registered with Osborne that the digital readout in the lower left corner of the screen was showing the current date with a time of 1:11 p.m. "Doc, it's for you," said Ray, handing him the cordless phone. "Marlene. She said it's urgent."

Osborne took the phone. "Yes—did you hear from Chief Ferris?"

"No, Dr. Osborne. But we have to reach her ASAP. I think you should drive out there right now if you can—" Osborne couldn't remember hearing Marlene sound so agitated.

"Has something happened?"

"After you left, I decided to listen to that 9-1-1 call that we got from Gwen Curry. It was nagging at me that I'd heard that lisping sound somewhere before, and recently, too. Dr. Osborne, I am sure she's the voice, the one with the 's' sound that we heard on the Universal Medical call—the one you thought was a man. That's Gwen Curry!"

"Marlene—you're sure?"

"Dr. Osborne, I hear voices all day every day and I *know* that is the same person on both those calls. Chief Ferris needs to hear this but I just tried calling her again and still no answer. This can't wait—"

"I'll take care of it right now, Marlene." Osborne turned to the group, the phone still in his hand, but before he could say a word, Mallory was pointing at the screen where Ray had started up the tape again.

"That's no deer, that *is* a person…I think. But what a strange shape. Who is that chubby person, Dad? Is that a friend of Lew's?" asked Mallory.

Osborne couldn't speak. The shape was too familiar.

He was on his feet. "That woman—that's Gwen Curry! And the call just now from Marlene makes me think she's the one who killed DeeDee Kurlander and Nora Loomis, not her husband! And now—now she's trespassing on Lew's property? She's *stalking* Lew!

"I have to get out there. Lew hasn't been answering her phone!" He was on his feet and running for the door.

Ray threw the remote onto the kitchen table, saying, "Take your car, Doc, but let me grab my gun."

"Mallory—call Laura on the switchboard." Osborne's voice was hoarse. "Tell her to get Roger and Todd out there right now."

In less than a minute, Ray had his rifle and was standing beside Osborne's car. He put up a hand and spoke loud enough that everyone could hear. "Slow down, folks. Stop right where you are. Doc, you, too," he said, grabbing Osborne's sleeve before he could open his car door. "We don't know what we're walking into, so let's all of us take a minute to think this through—"

"You're wasting time, Ray. What the hell else *can* we do!" demanded Osborne.

"I can tell you right now the last thing that should happen is all of us barging in there. Let's not set off someone we already know isn't thinking straight."

"Ray's right," said Gretel. "I'm no law enforcement professional myself, but I've done enough firearms training with people who have to be prepared to deal with situations like this and they always worry about hair-trigger reactions. My suggestion?" Gretel gave an apologetic shrug. "Take it slow, see what you're dealing with."

A moment of silence after she spoke, then Ray said, "Right. I suggest we take the back way in to the property and I know just how to do it—there's a logging lane that leads to a deer stand in the woods about four hundred yards from that deer garden, and it's another hundred yards or so to the farmhouse."

"Makes sense to me," said Mallory. "Dad, we were just out there setting up the cameras. Ray knows his way around—"

"Okay, but let's get going," said Osborne. "Mallory, Gretel, you two take Mallory's car—"

"One second, Mallory," said Gretel as Mallory ran toward her Jeep. "Let me grab my rifle from the trunk of my car." As she hurried toward her vehicle, Ray jumped into Osborne's car, cell phone in hand.

With Osborne driving, Ray called Laura back to tell her they were on their way out to Lew's and would be taking the back road in. "Laura," said Ray, "tell Roger and Todd to stay on the highway. Do not approach the drive down to Lew's place until we see what's happening there first…" He listened intently for a long minute then said, "Right. Tell Todd they need to keep traffic flowing on Highway 47 as if everything is normal. We do not—under any circumstances—want to alert the Curry woman that we think anything is wrong." Again he listened, then said, "Do *I* think anything is wrong?"

Osborne could see Ray struggling with too many answers to that question. He managed to say only, "I'm worried, hon. Real worried." He clicked off his cell phone and turning to Osborne, said, "What a time to have an amateur on the switchboard. Jeez, Louise."

THIRTY-TWO

CROUCHED ON THEIR KNEES in the woods near the tree stand, Osborne, Mallory and Ray waited and watched. They had pulled their cars to a stop halfway down the logging lane. Though the road was well hidden from the fields west of the farmhouse, Ray had insisted they walk in, and no one argued. No noise, no movement was the plan.

When they got to the deer stand, Mallory had said, "Should one of us pretend we think everything is okay and just walk up the driveway as if to check on her—"

"NO!" shouted Osborne and Ray simultaneously.

Gretel was kinder. "It's an option, Mallory, but if things aren't okay, you might ramp up the odds of getting Chief Ferris killed. Everything I've been hearing from you people about this Gwen Curry leads me to think she's a classic psycho—in which case she has nothing to lose."

"Gretel's got a point. Why would Gwen have snuck in here in the first place? What could she be thinking?" said Osborne, puzzling out loud. "She doesn't know that I know—not Lew, only me—that she is the one who killed DeeDee and Nora Loomis. So why go after Lew?"

"But what if she's hurt Lew already?" said Mallory. "What if she's been here, done something awful and gone?"

"That is exactly what I'm going to find out," said Ray.

"Can you do that without being seen?" said Gretel, worried.

"Yes." The grim determination in Ray's voice made it clear he would make it happen. "With these dark clothes on I can move through the pines and overgrowth along the lake, then up that berm behind the apple orchard and along the fence. The vines on the fence should cover me good enough. I can get within fifty feet of the kitchen window…"

"Here, Ray, in case you can't get that close," said Osborne, handing over the binoculars he'd grabbed from his car. Then Osborne, Mallory and Gretel watched as Ray slipped off, vanishing into the trees.

At first, the little farmhouse had appeared empty, but as the sun dropped low behind the pines, a light came on. Osborne saw movement in a clump of brush near the lighted window and held his breath. That had to be Ray. He hoped no one in the farmhouse had seen it.

Gretel tapped him on the shoulder and pointed up. Osborne nodded and reached to hold steady the make-shift ladder that led up the deer stand as Gretel pulled herself up and onto the platform, rifle under one arm. "Do you have everything you need?" asked Osborne.

"Don't worry about me. This gun of mine is a scope-sighted M-14. It's the best for long-range work and I'm damn good at that. All I need now is a target."

From below the deer stand, he watched as she knelt and shifted slightly to the left, to better aim toward the one lighted window. "Dr. Osborne," she whispered, "that window—am I looking into a bedroom? A bathroom?"

"No, no, that's the kitchen," said Osborne. A sudden murmur of voices from the farmhouse and Osborne shut up. A breeze from the east carried the voices their way. Osborne dropped to his knees, the better to see through the brush as he strained to listen.

"You were, too!" A voice dark with anger.

"That's Gwen…" whispered Osborne.

"Don't you… I'm in control here." Same voice but the wind swirled, muffling the words.

"I know that, Gwen," said Lew in a level tone that could be easily heard. Osborne exhaled with relief—at least she was alive. "I know you are in control. I respect that."

"You didn't…when you went after my husband." Gwen's words got lost in a shiver of pine branches. Her voice, when he could hear it, sounded so distant that Osborne wondered if she had her back to the window.

"I was doing my job—" Lew again, voice steady.

"No, you weren't! Just like that girl—you wanted him!" Hysteria bordered Gwen's accusation.

"Well…" Now Lew's voice faded into the wind, which had swirled to blow toward the farmhouse. Then, louder, "…is there anything I can do…"

"Oh—what would you *like* to do?" said Gwen, her words loud with challenge.

"What would I *like* to do?" said Lew. "If you let me, I would like to make one phone call to my daughter and my two grandchildren."

Osborne couldn't hear Gwen's response. But he did hear Lew's next words: "…and there's a man whose face I would like to see once more. But that's too much to ask, isn't it?" Her effort at a rueful laugh broke Osborne's heart.

A snort from Gwen, who said, "You're so easy. I have a question for you."

"Okay…" Lew sounded hesitant.

"Remember, I'm…"

"What did she say, Dad?" whispered Mallory.

"Don't know, I couldn't hear, either," said Osborne.

"Yes, Gwen, you're in control."

"…when I dump you off the end of that dock out there…"

Silence. Either Lew didn't answer or she couldn't be heard.

Mallory moved closer to Osborne. She said nothing as she slipped her arm through his and held tight. He put a finger to his lips.

"Well…" It was Lew speaking. "I imagine you'll enjoy watching."

"If she would just step in front of the window, I'd have a shot," whispered Gretel. "All I need is one shot—but she's standing off to the side somewhere."

With a slight rustle, Ray stepped out of the trees and knelt beside Osborne. He spoke in a whisper. "She's got Lew bound in one of the kitchen chairs with duct tape and the chairs trapped onto a dolly. She must be planning to wheel her off the porch and down to the dock like she said. It's four to five feet deep off the end of that dock—Lew won't have a chance.

"That's not all—the woman's got a handgun that she keeps waving. Gretel," Ray whispered, looking up into the deer stand, "how you doing up there?"

"I'm good. So what you're saying is if I see any

movement through that window, it has to be the Curry woman?"

"Right."

A SUDDEN FLASH of headlights caused everyone to look up and out toward the long, straight drive leading to the farmhouse.

"Who the hell?" said Ray, cursing softly. It was too dark to see the color of the car but Osborne could tell from the shape that it was a small sedan. Not one of the police cruisers.

"I hope that's not her daughter," said Mallory.

"Can't be," said Osborne, eyes riveted on the strange car. "Her daughter drives an SUV."

The car stopped in front of the farmhouse, the engine running. The door on the driver's side opened. A figure got out and crossed in front of the headlights: Marcy Kurlander.

"Hey! You!" bellowed a voice from inside the farmhouse. Marcy stopped short, illuminated in the wash of the headlights. "Chief Ferris, it's me, Marcy—I'm here about the Mass for DeeDee." She waved one hand in which she was holding something small and white.

A rifle shot, then silence.

"I'M OKAY. I'M OKAY." Lew's voice rang out across the fields. Marcy was through the door before Ray and Osborne had crossed the field halfway. They entered to find her tearing at the duct tape holding Lew's arms.

"Marcy," said Osborne, "whatever possessed you? You could have been killed."

"I had no idea anyone except Chief Ferris was here,"

said Marcy, looking up at them. "I brought this poem that I had printed up to hand out at the church during the funeral Mass tomorrow. I wanted to show it to Chief Ferris." She looked over at Lew, who was flexing her fingers and hands now that her arms were freed. "You're the only person I know who understands," she said. "I was feeling pretty down and thought maybe just talking to you for a bit might help so I decided to drive out. I should have called or waited, I know…" Her voice trailed off as she followed Osborne's gaze across the room.

Gwen Curry lay face forward on the kitchen table. Gretel's single shot had found its mark. The woman died instantly.

"This may not sound right," said Lew softly as she reached to squeeze Marcy's shoulders, "but I'm so damn grateful you were feeling bad."

THIRTY-THREE

HANDS GENTLE ON HER SHOULDERS, Osborne helped Marcy to her feet and handed her off to Mallory and Ray. He knelt, his eyes searching Lew's. "Are you hurt?"

"No, no, no. But I am so happy to see you!" She managed a smile.

"This was too close, kiddo," said Osborne, his voice hoarse and blinking back tears as his pocketknife cut through the remaining bands of duct tape binding her legs to the chair. However brave Lew tried to sound, her shirt was soaked with sweat.

"There—how does that feel?" said Osborne, when she was able to stand.

Shaking her arms, stamping her feet and giving her hands a brisk rub, Lew said, "That tape cut off my circulation." Flexing her fingers, she raked her hair back from her face, took a deep breath and turned to the five people watching with concern on their faces. Grinning, she said, "Hey, you razzbonyas—it's after seven! I expected you at lunchtime. What the hell happened?"

As everyone laughed in relief, Osborne said, "You tell us. I didn't get worried until around three o'clock when you weren't answering your phone."

"And *that* was two hours too late," said Lew with a snort.

"What *did* happen, Chief?" said Ray. "The minute we saw that woman's image on the FawnCam we were heading this way. You never saw Doc move so fast!"

"How the hell did she get to you? Didn't you see her crossing the field?" said Osborne.

"She caught me totally by surprise. You know I took the morning off, so I was in my vegetable garden, concentrating on picking lettuce leaves—I never even heard her come up behind me. Suddenly I have cold steel in my ear, look up, and guess who?

"Doesn't take brains to see when a .357 is loaded. And I had every reason to believe she had the safety off—so I knew right then I better just stay calm and take orders. How long has it been anyway? I feel like I've been in that chair for *days*."

"I wonder why we didn't see you on the FawnCam, too?" asked Gretel.

"Because the deer garden is on the other side of the farmhouse—it's Lew's way of keeping the deer out of her good vegetable garden," said Ray. "Six and a half hours?" Ray gave a puzzled look. "Why did she stay so long?"

"Why not? 'Chatty Cathy' had a captured audience—she was having a great time," said Lew, with a touch of grim humor. "She told me everything. God forbid I die thinking her husband was anything but a doofus. No, she was forthcoming on every detail of the scam that *she* orchestrated, not Hugh, over the last two years. She was quite proud of the fact they're wanted in at least three states. I have to admit—the woman was brilliant."

"And a bully. She had you pinned like a butterfly," said Gretel, "and enjoyed watching you squirm."

"Oh, yes," said Lew. "Finding me here made her day.

She wasn't expecting to, you know. She was planning to hide out until I got home after work. So when she found me—hey, she was delighted to take her time."

"Thank goodness," said Osborne. "If she had acted quickly—"

"But what was she thinking?" said Mallory. "Was she planning to kill you and then go back to selling on eBay? Figure no one would find out?"

"She was convinced she had us all fooled—*everyone,*" said Lew. "People like Gwen Curry think they're smarter than the rest of the human race." She added with a heavy sigh, "And that's what made it so hard to deal with her. She would not listen to reason…"

Eyes sad, she studied Gwen's still form where it lay across the kitchen table. "I can understand her fury over DeeDee Kurlander seducing her husband, but where did she get off thinking I was doing the same?"

"Is that what she said?" asked Osborne.

"Yes, she did. She accused me of coming on to him just like DeeDee did. Of course she's delusional, but where does that thinking come from?"

"You listened to the man," said Osborne. "With patience and respect. And she misinterpreted."

"I think you're right, Doc," said Lew. "That's certainly something she refused to do—or didn't want to do. Also, no question that couple was breaking up. You think she would take any blame for that? No. And the longer I'm in this job, the more often I deal with twisted minds—I'll never understand why these people think the way they do."

"Did she really think she would get away with killing you?" asked Osborne.

"No. She knew that the facts would come out, but she planned to be long gone by then. She didn't want to take the chance that someone in one of the cabins on the lake might see her drop me off the end of the dock, which is why she hung out here so long. She was waiting for after dark.

"The rest, to hear her talk, would be easy—just pack up her dog and head for the Canadian border. Said she had plenty of cash."

"Oh, gosh, the dog," said Mallory. "What do we do with the dog?"

"I'll take care of it," said Ray. "An old girlfriend of mine loves to take in stray animals."

Lew stood up and, hands on her hips, looked around the room. "I think it's time I stopped being a victim and took charge of things. Let's get Roger and Todd back to town. I'll call Laura and have the ambulance sent for Gwen."

"Wonder who we go to for information for the death certificate," said Osborne, reaching into his shirt pocket for his notepad.

"We'll figure that out as we go," said Lew. "Right now, if you'll excuse me, everyone, I have to call Wausau, arrange for the autopsy and see what they say about the situation here. It may be they'll want Dan Wright up here again."

"Lew—are we still on for fish fry?" said Osborne.

"Are you kidding?" Too late, Lew saw the twinkle in his eye. She punched him in the arm.

THIRTY-FOUR

"IT STARTED WITH LAURA," said Lew in answer to the question Ray had asked as the waitress delivered serving plates of blueberry pancakes, link sausages, eggs scrambled with ham and buttered toast to the long table in Kristine's Restaurant, Lew's favorite breakfast place. They had arrived just in time to get the last big table and everyone was there except Marcy, who had the funeral Mass and wake to prepare for. But for Ray, Mallory, Gretel, Doc and Lew, this was a great way to start a sunny Saturday morning, inhaling the aromas that filled the crowded little Three Lakes diner.

It was almost 9:00 a.m. They had all slept in after a night that didn't end until three in the morning. Dan Wright hadn't seemed to mind missing fish fry with his future in-laws, and with two colleagues had made it from Wausau to Lew's place within ninety minutes of her call. Still, even with his speedy arrival, the details of preparing the body for transport to the crime lab's morgue, interviewing everyone from Lew and Gretel to Mallory, Marcy and Doc, and then securing Lew's place had taken hours.

"Laura's young, you know, and she was so distraught after she got Mallory's call to send Todd and Roger for backup that she forgot protocol. So when

Marcy Kurlander stopped by and asked how to reach me with a written invitation to the wake for DeeDee—Laura handed her my home address. She assumed Marcy would drop it in the mail, not drive out to my house with it."

"How did she get past Roger and Todd is what I'm wondering," said Ray. "I thought those two guys were on the highway right outside the drive into your place, Chief."

"Oh, it was the usual Roger screwup," said Lew. "Todd was stationed about half a mile away watching traffic from the east. Roger was closer to my drive, but he decided to give some guy a ticket for going two miles over the speed limit so he wasn't paying attention to the road when Marcy came along and turned in. He never even saw her." Lew's shoulders slumped in relief as she said, "We are so fortunate that Marcy herself didn't get shot."

"Marcy and yourself," said Osborne. "Lewellyn, it's sheer luck that *you* are alive. Gwen Curry could so easily have shot you when she heard Marcy drive up."

Lew nodded. "I know. But what she did do was move across the room to look out the window, giving Gretel a target, thankfully. Although I wish the whole thing could have ended without losing another life." Lew sighed.

"Chief Ferris," said Mallory, "I can't stop thinking about those people—the Currys. They must have been having problems long before DeeDee got involved, don't you think? If I've learned anything in therapy since my divorce, it's that people split for reasons that have been simmering for a lo-o-n-g time."

"No doubt," said Lew, "but DeeDee's pregnancy is what convinced Gwen that Hugh was leaving her for good. No way was she going to let him run off with all their money and leave her behind as a target—the accomplice to the bank fraud."

"Did you know that when she showed up at your place? That she had shot her husband, that it wasn't a suicide after all?" said Ray.

"I should have but I didn't. Dan Wright had left messages on both my voice mails as he was driving out of town yesterday around noon," said Lew. "But that was after I checked my messages before going into the garden—and I haven't had time to replace my cell phone. Had I done so, I would have learned that the autopsy on Hugh Curry's body showed rope burns on both wrists, and other evidence that he died with his arms tied behind his back.

"But Gwen herself is the one who told me she killed DeeDee and Nora—Nora because she overheard that phone call and Gwen was sure the call could be traced to her. She was able to find her quickly because the poor woman had attended the job fair. She just looked up her address in the Loon Lake phone book."

"Lew, I could kick myself. I should have recognized Gwen's voice the first time we heard that tape," said Osborne. "It's unmistakable now. How could I have missed that? How could I have been so stupid?"

"Please, Doc," said Lew, "we're all human beings. When we see or hear things out of their usual context, they can be impossible to recognize. I've run into people from Loon Lake when visiting my daughter in Milwaukee, but not recognized them until they flagged me down. If you're not expecting to see something—you won't see it. That's why eye witnesses are the worst witnesses. Same with that call—we weren't expecting the

Currys. For that matter, you had only met them twice. And when you and I were meeting with them, we were listening for details, not voices."

"Chief," said Ray, spearing his third sausage link, "I'm curious as to how Gwen Curry caught up with DeeDee out at the campground, since I saw no sign of anyone forced into the area. Did she talk about that at all?"

"Oh, yes. The given is that DeeDee made the mistake of paying too much attention to Hugh when she thought Gwen wasn't watching—she was. Add to that Gwen's suspicions, not only of an affair, but she was pretty sure DeeDee had witnessed Hugh moving money out of several accounts. So Gwen was waiting for her to leave the Chamber office the other night—the night when DeeDee drove straight to Robbie's party. She followed her to Moccasin Lake, parked behind some boat trailers and waited. Her plan was to stay until DeeDee left the party, force her car off the road and attack her some-where on the way home.

"She was quite surprised when DeeDee returned to the parking lot so early that night. Right after her two friends drove off, DeeDee walked down to the camp-ground, which was out of sight from the public landing. Gwen, of course, followed her. Bert was waiting near a firepit and the two talked briefly. No doubt Bert was telling DeeDee once again that he had no intention of marrying her, because after he left, DeeDee stayed. She sat down on a log, crying. That's when Gwen showed up." Lew paused. "Poor DeeDee. Gwen hit her once with the muskie gaff and we know the rest, thanks to the Wausau boys.

"But Dan had an interesting piece of news that links

Gwen to both murders. Dog hairs found around the sites where Nora and DeeDee had been killed have been traced back to the Currys' dog. Very likely they came off Gwen's clothing."

"What about that muskie gaff?" said Osborne, the images of DeeDee and Nora's mutilated bodies vivid in his memory. "Any sign of it?"

"According to Gwen, it's at the bottom of Mirror Lake. She dropped it off the canoe. That is one time I do believe her."

"We'll never know, I suppose, but I've been wondering if she came upon us last night when we were at the barn? I thought I heard someone and then I saw a canoe paddling away," said Osborne. Noticing the jeweled rings on Gwen's fingers as the EMTs moved her body had caused him to remember the flash of light he'd seen outside the barn window.

"Say," interrupted Ray, "forgot to mention, my buddy Gunders and I—we found your kayaks with the fly rods still inside, you lucky dogs. A couple of soggy fishing vests, too. The life jackets floated quite aways but everything else landed pretty close by, believe it or not."

"My camera?" said Osborne, remembering Lew taking the photo of his trophy brown trout.

"No camera, Doc, sorry."

"Not to worry, Doc, we'll fish that stream again," said Lew, "with helmets."

"The big question I have," said Osborne, passing the maple syrup around the table to Mallory, "is where's the money? Where's all that cash that Hugh Curry withdrew from the banks?"

"Well, that was Gwen's doing, too," said Lew.

"Seems Wisconsin is the fourth state in which the Currys ran their scam so a number of banks and companies have been after them. No one has been able to find a money trail because they laundered it right away. They would take the cash, use it to purchase electronic goods of all kinds and Gwen would resell them on eBay. It didn't bother them if they bought at retail and sold at a discount because they got cash no one could trace.

"Nifty for them but it leaves our Loon Lake Police Department and three local banks with an old barn full of iPods, cell phones, computers, video games and who knows what."

"Mason will be heartbroken when she hears the truth about her hidden treasure," said Osborne. "I may have to buy her an iPod for her birthday."

"What *will* you do with all that stuff? Sell it on eBay?" Ray spoke as if that was the last thing anyone would do.

"Wait a minute!" said Mallory. "That's not a bad idea. Chief Ferris, the banks could hire Sharon Donovan to handle that. Even if they pay her a commission, they could get most of the money back. Cool stuff like that moves fast online."

"It's a good suggestion, Mallory," said Lew. "I have no idea how much red tape will be involved given that all the banks are sure to want a say in what happens to the goods."

Osborne pushed his plate away. "This was delicious."

"And deserved," said Lew. She gazed around the table and Osborne was sure he saw tears glisten as she said, "I,..um…I have to thank you all for being there for me." She straightened up and cleared her throat. "Ray, who knew you would save my life with that crazy video thing of yours."

"FawnCam," said Ray. "Thank your resident wolf—we were all hoping to see him—"

"Or her," corrected Mallory.

"And Gretel," said Lew. "I feel so bad I kept putting off meeting with you…"

"Guilt is a great sales tool," said Gretel. "Not to worry, I'll be back next month."

"Really?" said Ray. "Will you let me know when you're coming?"

"On one condition…" said Gretel.

"I know, I know—the jokes," said Ray. "I promise I'll put a lid on it." Mallory snorted.

LEW COULDN'T SLEEP at her place for at least another day.

"State law," Osborne had been pleased to remind her. "Last I heard someone died there under less than natural circumstances. Given how isolated your place is, Lewellyn, I've been wondering if you would consider moving in here…with me."

"I don't know, Doc. I love my place, even though what happened there leaves me feeling it's been violated. Why don't you give me…oh, six months to think it over?"

Lying beside her after they had decided to take a well-deserved afternoon nap, he smiled. "That's a nice way of saying 'no.'" Though all the windows were open, the day was hot and still. They had thrown both sheet and blanket off. Mike snored from his cushion near the door.

As Osborne was admiring what the glow of a summer afternoon does to a woman's body, Lew leaned over to kiss him…hard and harder.